HER NOBLE PROTECTOR

NIGHT STORM, BOOK SEVEN

CAITLYN O'LEARY

INTRODUCTION

Her worst nightmare had come true—somehow, she had been kidnapped and forced to kill her captor to get away.

Finally home in Arizona after a harrowing kidnapping, Lisa Garcia was scared all the time. She jumped at every sound and shadow, too scared to even leave her home. How could someone who used to ride the rapids and trek the wilds of Alaska be reduced to this?

Navy SEAL Raiden Sato had forgotten more missions than he could remember. But this last one would stick in his mind forever. Lisa Garcia. How could he ever forget her? Tough, strong, compassionate, beautiful, the woman was a force of nature. But Raiden couldn't help remembering how she'd been when they'd parted. She'd seemed broken. He needed to know how she was now.

When Raiden took leave to check on Lisa in Arizona, he was shocked at the woman he found. The kick-ass wilderness guide was gone, replaced by a woman still mired in trauma.

She was positive that someone was out to get her. Determined to help her, Raiden was positive that he could heal her with time, patience, and perhaps even love.

But what happens when Lisa is right, and somebody really is out to get her?

1

LISA SHOT UP, HER EYES WIDE AS SHE STRUGGLED TO BREATHE, struggled to get away, but something was holding her down. She tried to fight, tried to escape, then she heard glass shatter and it stopped her short.

She choked back a scream.

That was when saw the light on in her bathroom.

"Goddammit!" She was home. Here in her bedroom. She always kept her light on, so she wouldn't be scared if she woke up from a nightmare.

"Yeah, like that helped me."

This one was bad. She went to turn on the lamp on her nightstand. It wasn't there. She blinked back tears when she realized that was what the breaking glass had been; she'd knocked the lamp halfway across the room as she'd thrashed about. She yanked at the sweat-soaked sheet. The damn thing was tangled around her like some kind of jungle vine. She kicked herself free then swung her legs over the side of the bed, almost stepping in the glass.

Lisa crawled to the end of the bed, stumbled to the wall, and slammed on the switch so that the overhead light turned on. She whipped her head around and sighed in relief. The two locks on her bedroom door were secure.

God, what kind of loser has locks on their bedroom door?

"Shut up!" She heard her voice and realized it sounded weak. When was the last time she'd eaten? She closed her eyes, then opened them.

I'm pathetic.

The nightmare was probably nothing, but maybe she *had* heard something. She'd already called the police two times over the last seven weeks for no reason whatsoever—she wasn't calling again. She picked up the aluminum softball bat beside the doorframe. She slowly unlocked the door and waited.

And waited.

Her arms started to tremble. Lisa had no idea how long she'd been in this position, with the bat at the ready. Ten minutes? A half-hour? An hour?

She was afraid to move even a millimeter to glance at the clock on her nightstand. It wouldn't matter if she did, since she had no idea when she first stood watch.

You're such an idiot, Garcia!

She felt a tear slip through her defenses. The bat, which wasn't all that heavy, felt like it was made of lead. Lisa felt her right hand begin to cramp. When she tried to loosen her grip so that she could relieve the pressure, she couldn't get it to move.

She tried again.

Ahh God.

Now her tense shoulders were starting to tremble. She pushed herself against the wall, willing her body to move. She had to be able to swing the bat if someone came in. She *had* to.

She listened intently. She didn't hear anything, but that

didn't matter. She remembered how quietly the SEALs could move. She hadn't heard a thing when they'd come up behind the man who...who...

Lisa shook her head, willing the memory away. Willing all memories away, even the older ones that got confused with the newer ones. The ones with Damon. She pushed away from the wall and gritted her teeth. Willing away the tears.

I can do this. I can.

The bat started to lower as her shoulders lost strength. She rested the bat on her right shoulder; it wasn't good because she would lose some of her speed when she swung, but she had no choice. Lisa heard her harsh breathing. She needed to stop it—it would tip off whoever was out there.

Breathe through your nose. You can do it.

She kept listening intently. Nothing. Or was there something?

What is it? Am I going crazy? How long have I been in this position?

Her back hit the wall as she slumped, but so did the bat. The metallic *bing* rang through her bedroom as the top of the bat hit the tile floor. Somebody was sure to have heard it. She pushed herself off the wall and hefted up the bat, trying to get back to a batter's stance, but she couldn't, she just couldn't.

Her arms were trembling so bad that she could barely keep them up. Lisa tasted salt and knew she was crying again. She was always crying.

Staring at the doorknob, she willed it to move so she could take the swing before she fell over, but nothing moved. It was too much. With what little strength she had left, she grabbed the doorknob and swung open her bedroom door, and stepped out. The kitchen light was on, like it always was. Frantically, she looked around her home's open floorplan and saw nothing. She stumbled to the front door and sagged when she saw both deadbolts were in place and the cookie sheet was still leaned up against the door.

Her head swiveled on her neck as she spun to look at the door in her kitchen that led to her carport. Not only did it look closed, but she could also see that the pizza pans resting up against them were still in place. She whimpered with relief. She swung around again to check the patio door.

She was almost positive that nobody would have gotten in through her patio. They would have had to break the glass to get in, plus she had two cookie sheets and three pizza pans tipped up against that door, so they would've knocked them over and she would've heard the crash, but she lurched over to the door to double-check it anyway.

Lisa gave a watery sigh when she saw that the steel bar at the bottom of the sliding door was still in place and not one single pan had been tipped over. She felt her legs start to give out, and she eased herself to the floor before she fell down.

Lisa tried to drop the bat, but her hands were too cramped to let go. She shook her arms, trying to force it to drop on the floor. It finally fell. Her hands hurt like a son-of-a-bitch. She shoved them between her knees, trying to stop the painful tingling.

It was sweltering in her house; why hadn't she turned on the air conditioning before she went to bed? Looking around she wondered why she hadn't done a lot of things. There were dirty dishes all over her coffee table, and some on the floor in front of her couch. She frowned when she saw three bags of groceries on her dining room table. One was tipped over and there was a pint of yogurt and a loaf of bread peeking out. When had she ordered groceries? What was in the other two bags?

It didn't look like her house. This was not her beloved home. Another tear fell. What had her life come to?

Lisa rested her head against the blinds on her sliding glass door. It felt a tiny bit cooler. She should get up, right? She needed to keep her eyes open; if she didn't she'd dream then there wouldn't be a jungle, or the back of Damon's pick-up. The two times when she had been helpless. Utterly helpless.

Don't close your eyes.

Please God, don't let me close my eyes.

2

RAIDEN STOOD BACK AND WATCHED THE MENAGERIE. THERE were children everywhere, but somehow his mom and aunties managed to set the table with platters mounded with food, without tripping on one single toddler. He'd tried to help, but Auntie Rose had slapped his hand hard with a wooden spoon. At least it was his hand these days that got hit. He grinned as he took another sip of his beer. Out of the corner of his eye, he watched to see how his Lieutenant was handling things. So far, so good.

"Son, stop looking at the food and come to the garage, I want to show you something. Bring Max with you," his father yelled above all the noise.

"Absolutely not. All of you need to come to the table, the food is ready." Everybody stopped at the sound of his mother's emphatic tone. For a little Japanese woman, when she decided to take charge, she could definitely scare a Navy SEAL. He saw Max's right lip curl upward.

"Our honored guest will sit here," she said, standing behind the chair to his father's left and pointing at Max.

Mom was seated to Pop's right. Max no longer twitched when this happened; he was used to it. He'd been coming to the get-togethers for three years now, ever since Pop had found out that he liked old muscle cars too.

Max was just lucky Mom hadn't started to throw some of the single cousins his way. Of course, that would be pretty fucking funny. He must have caught on to Raiden's wicked thoughts because Max glared at him and ambled his way.

"What?" he asked.

"Nothing. Nothing at all," Raiden said with a grin. "Mom's waiting for you to sit down."

Max turned away from him, walked over to Raiden's mother, and gave her a kiss on the cheek. He talked to her for a moment and she was beaming after he was done. His lieutenant was a smooth talker when he wanted to be.

Raiden sat down near the end of the table next to his teenage cousin. Leif was sixteen and going nowhere fast. He'd been hearing whispers here and there about how the kid was doing in and out of school and it wasn't good. Leif's parents, God love them, were blaming it on the wrong crowd, but according to Raiden's mom and pop, his aunt and uncle were just letting the boy run wild. Then there was the info Raiden's younger cousin Willy had told him, which was *really* not good, so Raiden was pretty happy to be sitting next to Leif.

Leif was looking down at his phone, ignoring everybody. When the first plate came around to Raiden, it was filled high with Aunt Cindy's famous macaroni and cheese dish. He looked around the table and saw there was plenty to go around so he took a good-sized portion and asked Leif if he would like some.

"Leif?"

He sighed when the kid didn't answer.

Leif's fourteen-year-old sister Tallie was on his other side. She motioned for the dish and Raiden handed it to her.

"Leif?" she asked. He ignored her too. She scooped out some of the mac and cheese and smacked it down onto his plate. The boy still didn't look up from his phone. Raiden looked over at what the kid was texting.

GET ME THE CASH, AND YOU'LL GET THE ANSWERS Leif texted.

THAT'S TOO MUCH

THEN I GUESS YOU WON'T PASS THE CLASS

RAIDEN DIDN'T GET a chance to see how the person responded because someone just passed him the plate of Cousin Himari's famous karaage fried chicken, and he was damn happy to see she'd made a huge bowl. He took a healthy portion, then nudged Leif who grunted at him.

"Leif, do you want some chicken?" he asked. "It's Himari's."

No response.

"Leif?" he said louder, with another shoulder nudge.

Apparently, Tallie had had enough. She snatched Leif's phone out of his hand. "Quit being such a rude asshole," she hissed. "Raiden's asking if you want any chicken. He's asked you like four thousand times."

"Give me back my phone," he snarled. He made a grab

for it and spilled his water across the table onto Uncle Hideto, who was at least eighty years old. Aunt Hui was beside him, and both of them just shook their heads at Leif and murmured in Japanese about rude teenagers. Raiden passed the plate of food to Tallie and pushed back his chair, tapping Leif on the shoulder.

"Outside. With me. Now."

Leif's eyes widened. Raiden had been stuck babysitting Leif and Tallie years ago when he was in college. He made small talk with the boy when he was home for family functions, but now that he realized it, Leif had gone out of his way to avoid him and he should have sought him out long ago.

Out of the corner of his eye, he saw Auntie Kathleen start to stand up and he gave a brief shake of his head. She sat back down with a nod. She trusted him to handle things. He noticed that Leif's dad hadn't even bothered to try to get up, he just kept on eating. Meanwhile, Raiden's mom was grinning ear to ear. He rolled his eyes at her as he followed the kid to the front door.

As soon as they got outside, Leif pulled his vape pen out of his vest pocket.

"Nope," Raiden said. "You and I are going to have a little talk, so put that away."

"You need to mellow out," Leif sneered at him.

Raiden looked at Leif, really looked at him. He was a good-looking kid. The kid had a whole hell of a lot of things going in his favor. Looks, brains, doting parents, and some money.

Leif was almost as tall as he was. His hair was black like his mom's, but his eyes were blue like his Norwegian father's. The only real thing the kid had to bitch about in the looks department was his acne, but even that seemed to be clearing up from the last time Raiden had seen him, and if he'd bother to smile instead of having a surly-assed expression all the time, he might actually get a girlfriend.

Hell, then there was the fact that his parents thought sunshine shot out of his ass. They even bought him a brand new BMW when he turned sixteen. Raiden knew that because his Aunt Kathleen mentioned it every time anyone was within earshot. She also bragged that the kid was a straight-A student and did phenomenally well on his SATs. So why in the hell was he trying to fuck it all up?

"Let's take a walk," Raiden said as he started down the path to the sidewalk.

"Jesus, are we actually going to do this? Are you going to go all Mister Military on my ass and try to talk me onto the straight and narrow or some such shit?"

"Just move it along, Leif," Raiden said mildly.

"And if I say no?" Leif asked belligerently as he stood in the middle of the path.

"Then I'm going to see about blowing your ass out of the water, and make sure everybody knows what you've been doing."

Leif gave him a sideways stare, then gave a half-hearted chuckle. "You're not making any sense, but I'll walk with you if it will make you feel better."

Raiden waited until they were half a block down from his parents' house before he started talking. "So when did you start selling test answers?"

Leif caught the toe of his sneaker on a crack on the sidewalk and stumbled, then looked up at Raiden. "What are you talking about?"

"Makes me kind of wonder if you're really as smart as

Auntie Kathleen says, or if you just cheated your way through school."

Raiden watched as Leif's face flushed. "Who in the hell do you think comes up with the test answers?" he bit out.

"Beats me. Who?"

Leif's face almost turned purple. It was kind of fun baiting the kid.

"Who in the hell do you think you are, butting your nose into my life? You have no right! I've got my shit tight. I don't need some frogman or whatever you call yourself to come dictating to me."

"Seems to me you've got your kid sister dictating to you. Seems to me more people than me know what you're into. Seems to me that whatever scholarships and career you're angling for are going right down the toilet when you're caught, and believe me, you'll be caught."

"How do you figure that?"

"Fuck, kid, did you not see the college admissions take-down last year? Those people were pros. They got caught. People already have eyes on you, and it just takes one of your customers to blow the whistle. You trust every one of them to keep their mouths shut?"

He saw his cousin stop to consider what he was laying down. He might have half a brain after all. Then his eyes narrowed and he sneered. "I'm going to end up with ten times the money you have when I'm your age. I won't be wasting away risking my life for nothing. I don't think you give a shit what I'm doing; I think you're jealous."

Shit, why was he trying? The kid was showing all kinds of dickish moves. Still, he was family and Auntie Kathleen made a mean Ambrosia salad and she'd be heartbroken if sonny boy got expelled and got blackballed from college. Raiden blew out air and narrowed *his* eyes.

"I'm no longer asking, Leif. I'm telling. Your business is now officially shut down. Within two hours, every single one of your communication devices will be hacked and shut down. Anything you decide to start up, it will be shut down. Any burner phone, new computer that you purchase... Shut down. You're going to be dead in the water. You try to communicate through anybody else's device, I'll know... and your shit will be shut down."

Leif laughed. "Like that'll happen."

Raiden pulled out his phone, unlocked it, and pressed a number. He waited.

"Hey, Kane. Got a situation. Family's involved. Need a favor. Am I interrupting anything?"

Raiden listened to his second-in-command, Kane McNamara, who was their computer guru. He was also a world-class hacker from the time he was younger than Leif, and he had a hell of a software company that could accomplish anything. *Anything.*

"Nothing that can't wait," Kane replied. "So what do you need, Sato? You know you've got it."

"Thanks, I appreciate it. My little cousin is a sixteen-year-old shit who might be all that in the smarts department, but he has gone off the path, if you know what I mean." Raiden thought about telling Kane the kid was a dick, but he was family, so he refrained. Plus he was a kid, and hopefully with a little guidance and a kick in the ass he'd grow out of it.

"Who are you talking to?" Leif demanded to know. Raiden ignored him.

"Here's the problem. He's been selling test answers for at least the last year, and he's on the line to getting caught. He's going to blow his future out of the water. I need his entire online life shutdown, plus anything—and I mean anything—he might start or think about starting, shut down as well."

"Give me a name."

"Leif Johansen. He lives in Virginia Beach." Raiden supplied his aunt and uncle's address. "He's going to Princess Anne High School."

"Got it. He'll be shut down in an hour."

"Appreciate it," Raiden smiled.

"No problem. Is Max enjoying the food? Has your mom set him up yet?"

"Yes to the first, no to the second."

"Can't wait until she does," Kane chuckled. "Cullen and I have a bet on that."

Raiden laughed. "Thanks again."

"Later." Kane hung up.

Raiden looked at Leif and smiled. "By the time Tallie gives you back your phone, you'll be out of business."

"Yeah, sure," Leif smirked. "I'm sure you muscle types have it all covered."

"I'm going back in for food, you do what you want," Raiden said as he turned back toward the house.

"You know, everyone in this family thinks you're the shit. I don't buy it," Leif said as he trailed after him. "And I sure as fuck don't know why you're singling me out."

Raiden stopped and looked back at the teenager. "I'll tell you why. Family matters. Your parents matter, and you might not know this, but *you* matter. I might not have much respect or liking for you now, but I have hope. So you're worth my time and effort. Know this—I'll be keeping tabs."

Leif gave him a long, considering look. "Like I said, you're full of shit. You'll leave and won't even remember this conversation come tomorrow. Which is fine by me, because

I'll be back in business, and your stuck-up ass will be working out and playing soldier."

"And there's the attitude that makes you a dick. But like I said, I have hope."

Raiden meandered back to the house, in the mood for some of Aunt Kathleen's Ambrosia salad.

3

RAIDEN THREW HIS MUSTANG'S KEYS ON THE HALL TABLE
when he got home and picked up his mail. As much as he
tried to put Leif out of his head, he couldn't. He was only a
couple of years younger than some of the students he'd
helped to rescue seven weeks ago in Mexico, and yet it
seemed like they were a world apart. Some of them might
have started out as rich and entitled, but they'd stepped up.
Raiden had a real hard time thinking that Leif would be the
type who could and it hurt. How in the hell could he fix
this?

He flipped through the mail. All of it was going to hit the
shredder or the recycle bin. *What a waste of the world's
resources.* He headed to his kitchen and opened the fridge.
He tossed in the two Tupperware containers of leftovers that
his mom had packed for him. The ladies always cooked too
much, which he always appreciated.

Raiden started stripping as he headed to his bedroom,
then threw his clothes into the hamper. He pulled on a pair
of shorts and headed to the back room. He needed to get in
some PT; he'd drawn the short straw for tomorrow, so while

the others on his team were going to do Close Quarters Combat training, he was stuck doing paperwork. He desperately needed a workout, then a night run on the beach. By then he should have his head sorted.

He smiled when he got to the back room. It had taken more than a month to do the renovation, combining two bedrooms into one big room, so that it could actually fit enough equipment to work as a gym. First, he needed to spend time with the punching bag. He knew he needed to be more Zen about it, but his little cousin had gotten under his skin. After about a half-hour, he felt his shoulders and back loosen up and he grinned. Now it was time to get down to business.

He hit the rope fit trainer. He put the thing on the highest resistance and let loose. It still burned that he wasn't the fastest up the ropes on the team obstacle course. This piece of equipment had cost a pretty penny, but by God, it was going to be worth it.

Raiden was an hour into the training when his cell was ringing. He had a separate ring tone for team members, family, and his lieutenant. Call him anal, but it made life easier. He grinned when he realized it was Nic Hale calling. He'd been wanting to hear how young love was going. God, he couldn't be happier for him, especially now that Cami had started going to counseling. He was glad that talking to Carys had helped. Yet another special woman. His teammates were lucky.

He picked up his cell on the third ring, while he wiped sweat off his brow. "Yo, Nic."

"Hey. How you doing?"

Raiden smiled. Even Nic's voice sounded different—more relaxed, more tranquil, and if Raiden had to guess, at long last he was hearing and seeing the real Nic.

"Doing fine," Raiden responded. He was too, now that he'd let loose the Leif stuff and focused on the good family stuff. "What's up?"

"You know Cami started back up at William Mary, not full-time yet."

"Yeah, was really happy to hear that."

"Well, she started seeing students in her office. A lot of the kids from Mexico have been stopping by, and those that haven't, she's been reaching out."

Raiden thought about the last mission his Night Storm SEAL team had been on. They'd rescued a bunch of college kids from kidnappers in Mexico, seven weeks ago. A lot of them from William and Mary, Nic's high school sweetheart, Camilla Ross, being one of them. It had been hairy for those kids; he was happy that Cami was looking out for them.

"Not surprised." Raiden threw the towel over his shoulder and headed to the kitchen for a Gatorade.

"Here's the problem. She's been trying to get ahold of Lisa too."

Lisa had been the tour guide on the bus that had been captured by the kidnappers. She and Cami had stepped up to protect the younger students. They'd also taken the worst the kidnappers had to dish out.

Raiden stopped in front of the fridge, no longer thinking about a drink. "And what about Lisa?" he asked.

"Cami can't get ahold of her. Not a word. Kane's given her all the contact information, and nothing. Cami's even reached out to her old boss at the Wilderness Trekkers, and she won't say a word. You met her, right?"

Yeah, he'd met Paula Flood, the woman who operated Wilderness Trekkers. Raiden remembered her with wild red hair and the nicotine-stained fingers. She looked like she ate rocks for dinner. It had taken a half-hour in the waiting room outside Lisa Garcia's room at the hospital in Miami before she and Raiden had come to an understanding. Paula was fiercely protective of Lisa, even though she hadn't seen her in two years. He'd hated it when Lisa had been so adamant that Paula travel with her from Miami back to Lisa's home in Tempe, Arizona.

"Yeah, I met Paula," Raiden acknowledged. "Let me get this straight; Cami's worried about Lisa and she thinks that Paula has the info on how she's doing?"

"She's hoping that she's up in Alaska with her. According to all of Lisa's neighbors in Arizona, they haven't seen her."

Raiden took that in and realized that Kane must have been doing some super-sleuthing to get that information.

"I'll talk to Paula. I'll get her to talk."

"Thanks. Cami's really worried. She has a gut feeling."

And now Raiden did too. He had been worried about Lisa back in Miami. She was shut down. He'd seen that over in Syria and Afghanistan. Women who just weren't there anymore. But part of what Paula had said was that she had Lisa covered, and the Lisa she knew was a fighter and would bounce back. Nobody who'd volunteered on the Juneau Alaska Mountain rescue crew could ever be stopped. Raiden prayed Paula had Lisa under her wing.

"WHAT DO you mean you haven't talked to her in five weeks?" Raiden said softly. He worked hard to keep it together as his hand damn near crunched his phone into pieces.

"My daughter ended up leaving again, I've got my three grandkids living with me." He could hear the struggle in the older woman's voice. He tried to care, but he was having a hard time.

"Why didn't you call her family?" Raiden demanded to know.

"She doesn't have any. Nada. Zilch."

Raiden struggled with that answer; he just couldn't imagine it since he was surrounded by family.

"How about other friends? Colleagues?"

"Raiden, Lisa has a whole crew of acquaintances, but she doesn't have people that will pick up everything and go to her. That's not how she operates. All of her time is spent working at some charity down in Arizona. Something to do with foster kids. I don't know, she's told me. But I can't remember."

"Fine, there was only you, and you weren't available. What'd I tell you? I told you if you needed back-up, you call me."

"I talked to Lisa in the hospital; you are no one to her," Paula said. "Sure, you and your team got her out of hell, but she wasn't having any part of any of you." Paula's voice softened. "Raiden, she's hurting, and I don't think any man's presence is going to be welcome."

"I get that, but she isn't taking Cami's calls. Not returning texts, nothing. She was in that hell with her. They were partners, they kept it together and helped keep those kids safe. You say it's been five weeks, have you left messages? What have you done since then?"

"I've left messages."

"And has she returned them?" Raiden persisted. "Has she texted you? E-mailed you? A smoke signal? Any goddamn thing?"

"Her phone goes straight to voicemail, and her voicemail is full. I've texted her a million times, and nothing, nada."

"Why didn't you show up at her door?"

"I can't leave my grandbabies. I'm stuck here." Now Raiden could hear the sorry in the woman's voice. It was not going to do one damn thing to help the situation Lisa was in.

"Again, you should have called me."

"What could you do that I couldn't?"

"Don't worry, Paula. I'm on it." He said it firmly, hoping she'd feel a little bit of relief.

He could hear as she sucked in deep on a cigarette. "Thing is, you're not the right person for this. No man is."

"I'm on it. It'll be okay." He said it softly. He said it reassuringly. He knew Paula needed both. She was in a tight situation and she needed kindness right now, life was biting her in the ass and she was one of those types who was always trying to do for others. He let her know that he had her back. "I'll take care of your girl."

"Do you promise?" she asked, her voice just as soft.

"Absolutely. I'll call with updates."

"Thank you, Raiden."

He hung up and made his next call. Since he needed Max's support he sure as hell hoped that his mother hadn't tried any blind date shenanigans.

"Hey," Max answered. "Thanks again for the invite. I've got enough leftovers to cover me for three days."

"Not surprised, you were the guest of honor so you got the most," Raiden chuckled.

"The red bean mochi is out of this world. I need to get that recipe."

Raiden knew he wasn't kidding. Max cooked.

"Mom doesn't give out recipes. She doesn't have anything written down. You have to go over and she shows you as she makes it."

"Sounds like a hoot. I'm game."

Raiden smiled. Yep, there was a lot to like about Max Hogan. "I need to ask for a favor. I know it's last-minute, but I need leave."

"Something wrong? Do you need help?"

Again, there was a lot to like about this man.

"I don't need help, at least not yet. Remember Lisa Garcia, the tour guide from the Mexico mission?"

"Sure."

"Nic's Cami can't get ahold of her."

"And you were the last one to leave Miami because you were staying behind until someone showed up to claim her. I remember. Kane told me you had people getting you information on her, and the only person she had was an old boss, that right?"

"You remember all that?" Raiden asked.

"Raiden, when one of my men takes two additional days to stay with one of our mission victims, yeah, I'm going to remember. I'm even going to ask some questions because we've worked together five years. This is so far out of normal for you, that it is not in the same galaxy. Tell me what's going on."

"Lisa has been off the grid for five weeks now. Not a peep. Paula, the boss, left her in her house in Tempe. Due to some of her life getting in the way, she hasn't stayed in touch. Neighbors haven't seen her. She's not communicating with anyone. Cami's getting frantic."

"I could see that. And you?"

Raiden did a gut check. He wasn't frantic, but worried? Yeah, worry was one of the emotions roiling around inside him.

"I'll cop to worried. Maybe more. I'll know when I see her."

"Raiden, it wasn't easy for her down in Mexico. It was

worse for her than Cami. Can you cope with that?"

"Yes, Max. Yes, I can."

IT WAS early December in Arizona. Raiden didn't know a whole hell of a lot about plants, but he did know if a plant had died of neglect or not, and he was looking at an entire porchful of brightly colored pots of dead neglected flowers. He touched one dried bud and it disintegrated at his touch. He looked up and saw the blinds on either side of the door shut tight. Tighter than tight. He couldn't imagine one ray of sunshine penetrating.

The big picture window that had to be for the living room was the same way. It almost looked like something had been shoved along the windowsill ensuring nobody could look in, or out.

Raiden debated how to start out. Ring the bell? Knock soft? Call out?

All of the above?

First, he tried the door. There was only a 99.9999 chance it would be unlocked, but he had to try. It was locked.

Raiden rang the doorbell and knew he'd be waiting in vain. He'd already called her cell phone countless times, but always went straight to a full mailbox. The texts showed that they were delivered, but who in the hell knew if she'd read them.

He waited three whole minutes, then rang the doorbell again.

Nothing.

He'd gotten into Tempe late last night and checked into a budget motel. There was no way he was going to arrive on her doorstep after dark; he'd really hoped that at ten in the morning he'd have more of a chance to get her to open up. He knocked on the door—softly, but loud enough to be heard.

He waited three minutes.

Nothing.

He knocked again, harder. He looked around the neighborhood. It was older; if he had to guess it had been built in the Eighties. Her tidy little stucco house was set back at the end of a cul-de-sac. It wasn't as if the neighbors had a clear view of her front porch, but still, he was reluctant to just keep ringing and knocking. He stepped back a few steps and did even more of an evaluation of the house than he had walking up.

One-story rambler—kitchen, dining room, and living room up front. Those were easy calls. Carport to the side, with a door. He'd have to check that. Ford F-150 underneath. To really get a feel, he'd have to peruse the sides and back to get a sense of the rest of the place. Shit, maybe he *should* have come around last night, it would have made his reconnaissance a little easier. He took one last look around the neighborhood and made up his mind.

He went over to the carport. No doorbell, so he knocked. He was a little more out of sight, so he called out.

"Lisa? Are you in there? It's me, Raiden Sato. I was with you in the hospital in Miami. Do you remember me?"

He waited, and as he expected, there was no answer.

Casually he went around the little path through her low water maintenance front yard made up of a lot of rocks and succulents. He got to the tall gate attached to the fence enclosing her backyard. He reached over to unlatch it and found that it was padlocked. By the heft of the lock, it was heavy-duty.

Hmmm, was it new?

The fence might be high, but nothing higher than what he encountered on the obstacle course. He was over it in seconds. He glanced at the padlock. Yep, it sure looked brand new. He took his time walking through the landscaped backyard. Again, it was low water maintenance, and it looked good the way she had it laid out.

There was a small patio with a pergola over it. She had quite the set-up, but it was for one person, not a party. One big comfy padded chair and ottoman in the shade, a nice teak table beside it, with an upside-down book resting on it. There was a lounger that wasn't in the shade, also nicely padded, another low table beside that, no book.

Raiden scoured the back of the house. Little window over an exhaust vent, so that was the laundry room. Beside it was a good-sized window that he figured was the guest room. Then there was a much bigger window which he would bet his bottom dollar was the master bedroom. On the end was a small window up high. Master bath. Every single one of them closed up tight. He saw the a/c unit running beside the house, which told him that her electricity was still on and she was home. At least she was staying cool in the pitch black, which meant she was still taking care of herself, at least somewhat. But...

Goddammit!

He pinched the bridge of his nose. Raiden took a deep breath in the hot arid desert air—at least he was used to that. He could suck it down for months and not have it bother him. There were a couple of bottles in his car, along with some protein bars, but he'd have to get some supplies in order to carry out his plan.

There wasn't a chance in hell that he'd let this stand. Raiden headed back to the padlocked gate. It was time to get serious.

4

LISA RESTED THE BAT BESIDE THE FRONT DOOR AS SHE watched Raiden's rental car back out of her driveway through the peephole. Despite the now-cool air in her house, she was drenched in clammy sweat. During the day she kept her bedroom door open and she'd heard it when the car pulled up. It had taken all of her willpower not to run to her bedroom and throw the deadbolt. She had to find out who was at her door. She wasn't expecting any deliveries, but it could be something else that she would have to deal with. That she'd *have* to deal with.

Her worst nightmare was Paula sending the cops to do a welfare check. That was the reason she needed to be able to meet them on her porch. Upright. Breathing. Not let them into her house. That would be enough, wouldn't it?

But instead of cops, Paula had sent *that* man. Why in the world would she have sent Raiden Sato? Lisa lifted a trembling hand to her lips. She felt her breath wheeze out in relief. It didn't matter, he was gone now.

But he'd looked around. Poked into her business. He'd left her porch and knocked on the carport door. Called out to her. She was pretty sure he'd gone into her backyard. Why?

He's gone now. I'm okay.

Her laugh was more a broken sob.

Yeah, sure I'm okay.

She reached over to grab the bat but her arm had no strength, and only one finger ended up touching it. It clanked onto her tile floor. She cringed at the loud sound.

Lisa bent down slowly and picked up the bat. It dragged against the tiles as she headed to her bedroom. Sleep. She just needed some sleep.

This time when she crawled into bed she took the bat with her, not knowing if she would wake up in the afternoon or night. She looked at the clock on her nightstand and saw that it was eleven-thirty. She noticed her Garmin tactical watch beside it. Glancing down she was stunned to see it was mid-December, how was that even possible?

The kids. She wasn't going to be there with the kids for Christmas. She always had gifts for them. Always. She was going to miss everything. Everything was done. Everything had been taken away. She gripped the bat harder, resting her head against the tape-covered handle.

Please don't let me dream.

LISA SHOT UP and something hit her jaw hard. She scrambled backward, trying to get away from whoever was hitting her. She kicked out and her shin hit something metal. Her head swiveled around when she heard the gentle tapping against her bedroom window.

"Lisa, can you hear me? It's me, Raiden Sato," the voice said gently.

How could a man's voice be gentle?

Lisa shoved against the metal and realized it was her aluminum softball bat and shoved it out of her bed.

"Lisa?"

She scuttled backward on her heels and butt until her back hit her headboard. He was right outside her window. How did he get there? What did he want?

"Lisa, I just want to know if you're all right. I promised Paula that I'd call her. Will you talk to me?" His voice was so soft and gentle. Was she dreaming it? She locked her arms around her shaking knees.

For a long time, he didn't say anything, so maybe he was a dream, but she still couldn't stop shaking. Wait a minute, she was rocking. Her legs hurt. Her arms hurt. Maybe he'd gone away.

"Honey, will you answer me? I'm worried about you."

She gripped harder and pain seared up her shoulders.

Please, won't he just go away? Please.

"I hope I'm not scaring you. That's the last thing I want to do. You never deserve to be scared. If Paula could come, she'd be here, I hope you know that."

She shook her head. Back and forth, until long dark tendrils stuck to her cheek and mouth. Now she couldn't see. The black made her heart shudder. She unlocked one arm and smeared the hair out of her face. He'd said something else while she'd been shaking her head, but she hadn't heard him.

"That's why she can't make it. I hope you can understand. She'd love it if you'd call her and let her know you're safe. Can you do that, Lisa?"

Lisa glanced over at her nightstand, the one that used to have her pretty lamp on it. She'd thrown her cell phone in it after she'd turned it off. The cell phone that had been with her in the jungle.

Her hand clutched her throat. She couldn't breathe. She tried to suck in air, but it wouldn't work.

The drawer of the nightstand narrowed until it was all she could see.

She gasped. She needed air, but there wasn't any.

The cell phone was in the drawer trying to reach out and get her.

Where was the air?

Her head hit the headboard and she saw her ceiling fan; black dots were whirling around in front of her eyes. No air.

I've got to breathe. I'll die if I don't breathe.

She felt herself sinking. The black was taking over; would there be nightmares in the black?

"THE VIEW of the sunset out here is amazing. Is that why you bought this place?"

Huh?

She heard a man's voice from far away. It hurt her head. Her bathroom light was on, she could see that all of her bed covers, including the sheet, were on the floor. Her pajamas stuck to her body, and when she touched her temples to try to stop the pain, she felt the grease in her hair.

"I'm going to use your lounger to sleep out here tonight."

What?

Lisa blinked hard, trying to remember. He'd been here at ten o'clock this morning. She looked at the clock, it was six at night. She remembered he'd gone away, he must have come back.

Raiden.

Raiden Sato.

Asian. Big. He'd been big in Miami, while she'd been in the hospital. Muscles. His hands were twice the size of hers. He'd scared her at first, but those warm brown eyes with his high cheekbones had gotten to her. And his smile. How could a man who was a soldier have such a tender smile?

She'd asked him to go. He'd left her hospital room, but he never really left. She'd felt his presence outside, and after a while, his presence made her feel safe.

Maybe this time he'd really leave.

She moved over to the other side of the mattress and went to put her feet on the floor. That's when she realized the shards of glass were still there. She couldn't walk to the window.

"Go away." Her voice was husky from disuse. She knew he couldn't have heard her.

"What did you say, honey?"

Lisa swallowed. "Go away." Her voice was louder.

"I can't do that." Still gentle, his voice even sounded kind. He was disagreeing with her. He wouldn't do as she asked, but he sounded kind. It made no sense.

"Go away, Raiden." She put the firm in her voice.

"You remember me; that's good, honey." Now she heard the smile in his voice. So many nuances.

Lisa rubbed at her temples again. Her head was throbbing, her hair was greasy, and her clothes were sticky. She probably smelled but she couldn't notice since she'd gotten used to it. She'd been here too many times to count. She had to get to the bathroom and her Tylenol. Maybe even a shower. He'd be gone by then.

A woman could hope.

Lisa crawled to the other side of her mattress, got up on wobbly legs, and made it to the bathroom. She filled her glass with water and poured three pills out of the mega bottle of Tylenol and downed them. She grimaced; the water out of the tap was kind of brackish, but walking to the kitchen for bottled water—if she even had any—seemed insurmountable. She tried to remember the last time she ate and couldn't come up with anything. She had to eat, but the thought of it made her stomach twist in revolt.

She tried to pull her pajama top over her head, but she got dizzy. She stopped and moved two steps so she could rest her butt against the sink, then tried again. It worked. It took two tries to take off her pajama bottoms and when she was done she was shivering. She stumbled to the shower and turned the water on, setting it to hot.

By mistake, she caught a glimpse of herself in the mirror and slammed her eyes shut. Reaching into the stall, she felt the heat of the water and climbed in, hoping that the shower would help wash away all of her feelings. She didn't want to feel anymore. She didn't want to think anymore, or notice the changes in her body. Fine, she looked like she'd been in a prison camp, but what did it really matter?

Lisa noticed the loofah beside her favorite peach body wash. It was next to a pear scent, but that wasn't right, she never used pear. She squirted some peach onto the loofah and gagged.

That night. The faint smell of peaches on my skin.

Her eyes watered as bile filled her mouth. She pushed at the shower door but wasn't in time to get to the toilet. She spit vomit into the shower.

The smell of vomit and peach made her gag again. She stumbled to the toilet and wretched into it. She remembered El Jefe slicing her arm open. Lisa slapped her hand over the scar, feeling the pain, remembering the blood. The smell of copper, body odor, and peach all mingling to forever drive home a soul-deep terror. She continued throwing up until there was nothing left, but there hadn't been much to begin with.

Somebody was crying but Lisa couldn't figure out who. They sounded so sad, and she wanted to help them. When she opened her eyes she saw her red bathroom mat.

"Jesus."

She rolled over on the rug and looked up at the ceiling, shivering and crying. She flashed back to that time in Mexico, replaying it when the kidnapper had grabbed her and calmly sliced his knife into her arm, laughing while he did it. Just to prove a point to the other prisoners. She could still feel that first sharp pain as the knife pierced her flesh, then the knife tearing through her skin as it went from bicep to elbow, and that wasn't the worst of it.

She swiped at her tears and pushed her aching, shivering body up off the floor, using the sink counter to help her. The shower was still running; she saw steam coming out. No vomit on the floor.

"Get clean, Garcia," she gritted out to her reflection. "And whatever you do, don't use the peach soap."

For a moment, just an instant, she saw a smile on her face. Who knew that she could smile?

"Get in the shower. Get warm! Get clean!"

When she stepped into the shower stall she picked up the loofah and ignored the bottle of peach soap on the floor. She grabbed the pear soap and loaded up the loofah, breathing in the new scent. Her stomach didn't object. For long minutes Lisa soaped her body. She no longer tried to scrub away her skin like she had weeks ago. That had been useless and just made her bleed. Now she just soaped and cleaned herself, always ignoring the ugly red scar on her arm.

Grabbing the pear-scented shampoo she worked to keep her eyes open as she washed her hair. Pushing her fingers through her hair and massaging her scalp felt good. She poured a second helping of shampoo into her hand and started again, then froze.

She hadn't locked her bedroom door!

Lisa ducked her hair under the water, shaking her fingers through the strands to get rid of the shampoo. Even before she was done, she shoved open the shower door and raced out of the bathroom, then slammed her bedroom door shut. She fumbled with the locks but was finally able to thrust the deadbolts closed. Leaning against the door she jumped when Raiden started talking.

"Are you all right? I heard a crash. Talk to me, Lisa."

He sounded concerned. Worried.

Even with her bedroom door locked, Lisa felt utterly exposed as water dripped off her naked body. She pushed off the door and grabbed up a blanket to cover herself.

"Lisa, talk to me. Are you all right? What happened."

She wound the blanket around her body twice, the second time so it could cover her head and shoulders. Looking around she spotted her dresser and the little spot between that and her wall. It was a safe little space that she could tuck herself into. Lisa stumbled across her room and dropped down into a small huddle.

"I'm worried. Tell me what happened. I don't want to come in without an invitation, but you're scaring me."

"Don't come in." Her throat hurt after the vomiting. She realized he couldn't have heard her words, she tried again. "I'm fine. Don't come in."

"What happened?" he finally asked.

Lisa dropped her forehead onto her knees. She didn't

want to answer. She didn't want to talk. Hadn't she said enough?

"Honey, are you okay?"

She shivered. The control to the air conditioner was out in the living room and her bedroom was way too cold. Her wet hair was making her even colder. The duvet looked like it was a million miles away.

"You've got to say something, or I'm going to come in."

She heard the worry in his voice.

"Please don't come in," she begged. "I slammed my bedroom door. Don't come in. Promise me."

He didn't reply and she stared at the window, willing him to answer. Willing him to promise.

"Lisa, I'm worried about you."

"Don't worry about me. Just promise me you won't come in. Promise me." She hugged the blanket tighter around her.

"I promise. I won't come in unless you ask me to."

Lisa's shoulders sagged in relief. She shivered again.

Get up. Get up. Get up.

She pushed against the wall to get to her feet. She needed to dry her hair. There was some juice in the fridge. Maybe some Sprite. Crackers. Anything. She didn't recall eating for days. She could turn off the air conditioning. She took a small step toward her door.

"I started the book you were reading. I really like it."

Lisa spun around so fast that she had to grab the dresser before she fell down.

What? What did he just say?

"I haven't read Orson Scott Card before, he's good. Do you read a lot of science fiction?"

She tried to grapple with what he was saying while she held the blanket to her without falling down.

What is he talking about?

"I told you to go away," she husked out.

"I told you I wasn't going to do that, honey." Still tender. Still gentle.

She needed to make it to the living room to turn off the air conditioning. She needed Sprite. She needed crackers. Making it to the door, she slumped against it and her trembling fingers finally worked open the locks.

The thermostat control was way over near the couch. Food first. She heaved a deep sigh and made it to her kitchen. The sour smell coming from the bags on her dining room table was noxious, but she held her breath as she went by. She'd bought yogurt. Something else too that'd gone bad. Pulling the fridge door open took more strength than it should have, but at least there were green bottles inside. Her eyes teared up with relief.

A sleeve of saltines was open on the counter, so she knew they'd be stale. She opened the cupboard and pulled out the box and found a fresh sleeve. She carried her bounty to the couch and changed the temp in the house to eighty. Pulling the throw from the back of the sofa onto her feet, she opened her bottle of Sprite and took a long swig. The relief was immediate. Her stomach began to settle. Lisa leaned her head back against the pillows on her couch and sighed, then she put the bottle between her knees and wrenched open the crackers and sucked some of the salt off the cracker.

Heaven.

She bit into the cracker and realized she was hungry. Six crackers later, and half a bottle of Sprite and she started thinking. There was a man in her backyard. Not just any man, but a SEAL named Raiden Sato.

Lisa rummaged around her brain, trying to get a handle on what she thought about that, but she couldn't. She put her soda and crackers on the floor and pulled her knees up, then rested her head on them. She needed to think. Her tummy felt a little bit better. Her gaze drifted around her house and her eyes watered.

It wasn't her house. *Her* house was clean and it smelled good. Her house had the blinds open and... and... she liked it. She didn't like it here. It was scary here, even though it was the only place that felt safe.

Her lip trembled at that thought; how could her home be scary and safe?

It's not your house, it's your head. Your head is scary.

More tears followed that thought.

She tried to remember a time when she wasn't scared. When had she felt her absolute best? Tugging the blanket tighter around her, she looked at the painting on her wall. It was of the Hubbard Glacier in Alaska. She'd been there. She'd hiked there. Wild and gorgeous, it had always spoken to her soul. Could she really live a life without seeing it again?

She kept staring at the picture, then thought of her job in Mexico, sure she would find some of her father's family. She'd been wrecked when she found that all of her father's relatives were dead and buried. It was like she had nothing. No real past, no future, nothing.

She jerked her head up when she realized she'd closed her eyes again. No sleeping. She couldn't let herself dream. Dreams were bad. She touched her hair and felt that it was drying, so that was good, and she wasn't shivering anymore. Bending down, she grabbed the Sprite and crackers so she could have some more.

"You've been quiet a long time in there. Do you feel like talking?"

Lisa jerked and Sprite spilled on her blanket. Raiden's

voice was still that smooth and gentle rumble, but this time it was laced with worry. And, he was right outside her sliding glass door. Maybe three feet away from her. She saw a small empty spot on her cluttered coffee table and put the soda bottle on it. She leaned over and pushed back one of the blinds, then yanked her hand back.

She'd seen his arm. He was standing right there! Her heart hammered in her chest. A million miles a minute. A man was right outside her house and she'd told him to leave and he hadn't gone.

"Go away!" She heard herself. It was a cross between a shriek and a plea.

"Ah, Lisa, please don't be scared. Paula sent me, remember?"

A picture of Paula flashed through her brain. Red hair, generous smile, eyes that saw into your soul. Paula was safe.

"Paula wouldn't send you. She'd come herself."

"She couldn't, honey. Her daughter dumped off her three grandbabies. She's got to take care of them. She wanted to be here so bad, but she couldn't."

Lisa pictured Paula's daughter, a strung-out loser who had been going downhill since she turned twenty and popped out her first kid while addicted to meth. No matter how many times Paula got her into rehab, it never stuck. Maybe this time she'd get custody of her grandchildren for good.

"You can't be here. I don't want you here. I'm fine by myself." Lisa began to shiver again, even though it was now warm in her house.

"Honey, you're not fine."

Lisa didn't know how to respond to that. She looked around her house and knew he was right, but nobody could help her, so he needed to go away. Now.

"Please, Raiden, please go away. You're scaring me." That was the God's honest truth.

It was as if she could feel his wounded energy coming through the patio door. "Do you really think I would hurt you? Really?"

Lisa nodded her head into her knees. She thought back to the big man she had met in Miami. Then her mind flashed back further to the man in Mexico. The man who had touched her so gently. The man who had talked to her in a soothing voice and told her it would be all right, that she was safe, and he would take care of her. *That she was safe.* That's why she'd never screamed when she heard his voice outside her window, because she recognized Raiden from before, and he had kept his promises.

"No, Raiden, I don't think you would hurt me. You helped me."

"Thank God for that."

"But having you here, having you talk to me. It's too much. I can't handle it."

"Honey, I've never been in your shoes. All I can say is, if I could take your pain away, if I could've had it happen to me instead of you, I would change places in a fucking heartbeat, but I can't."

Lisa gasped in a deep breath of air. It sounded like he meant it. Like he really meant it.

"Lisa, I've been around a lot of people, both men, and women, who have gone through some devastating shit in their time. Some have come through to the other side, and some haven't. Do you want to know what made the difference for every single person who made it through to the other side? They had people they could rely on, and they reached out."

"But I still don't understand why you're here, Raiden. Why you? Why do you care about me?"

"I care because I care. I saw you in Mexico, I know how hard you fought to keep those kids safe. I know you were the one who kept her head and called in when the bus was first captured. Your bravery astounded me. Then I saw you in that hospital in Miami, I saw you hurting. No woman deserves to be hurt like you've been. It broke my heart, Lisa. I wanted to be there for you. You touched my heart. I'm here because I think you need me, and I don't want you to be one of those people who doesn't make it to the other side."

She didn't know how to respond. It was too much. Her eyes drifted back to the picture of the glacier.

"Did you hear me?" Raiden finally asked.

"I heard you. I need to go to sleep now," she said quietly.

"Okay, honey."

5

Raiden had left for his crappy motel that night and showered, then picked up some supplies on his way back to Lisa's house. He'd talked to Max and knew the team was out on a short mission. He felt like shit that he was missing it, but Max told him to cool his jets. Then Raiden called Nic, wanting to know how Cami was going to be handling her first time without him after the kidnapping. He wasn't surprised to find out that he'd insisted she stay with one of their teammate's wives. Carys Lyons was a doctor who had also gone through something traumatic, and was a perfect person to ensure that Cami could cope.

"Cami's less than thrilled about it," Nic had said on the phone. "Said she didn't need a babysitter, and that if I thought she was that young, maybe we shouldn't be having sex."

Raiden had laughed at that. Camilla Ross sure could be a spitfire.

After his shower and calls, he'd hauled his ass back to Lisa's house as fast as he could and now had her patio set up to his satisfaction. The backpack cooler was a hell of a lot better than anything he'd ever had overseas. He had a lounge chair, a sleeping bag, food in the cooler, and more than enough time on his hands to wait out one scared woman. He just hated that he had to do that.

Dammit.

He looked up when he heard a thud inside what he was sure was the living room. It was farther away than where she had been before.

"Lisa?" He called out.

Nothing.

"Lisa?" He was louder.

"Lisa!" He shouted.

Still nothing.

He banged on the sliding glass door.

He didn't let up. What in the hell was that thud, and why wasn't she answering? Was it time to break in? He really didn't want to. She needed coaxing. Raiden knew deep in his gut that had to be his approach, and anything else would betray her trust. He desperately needed her trust. And he knew, deep in his gut, she needed someone that she could trust.

"Raiden?" he heard her whisper softly. He rested the flat of his hand against the sun-warmed glass.

"I'm here, honey. Did you fall? Did you hurt yourself?"

"I'm a'right."

She didn't sound all right. She sounded punch drunk.

"Lisa, come back near me. Lay down on the couch where we can talk."

"Can't, need to put on clothes."

He sucked in a deep breath. She was wandering around her house naked?

"Go get dressed and come back to me, yeah?"

"'Kay."

He didn't go back to her bedroom window; it felt like he would be invading her privacy. His fingers fanned through the pages of the book. He was halfway done. Tonight, when Lisa was asleep he'd probably finish it. He hadn't been kidding her, it was damn good. Seeing the type of books she liked told him something about her, something good, substantial.

Raiden sat down on the edge of the chair with his elbows on his knees and waited. It was quite a bit of time before he heard any noise.

"You settled?" he asked.

"Kind of," she answered. "So you're here for round two? How many days are you planning on staying?"

She sounded curious. Curiosity was good.

"As many as I need to."

Her sigh was audible. Raiden decided not to say anything, just wait her out.

"I still don't get why. Why?"

"Lisa, you're good people. You're in trouble. I'm here to help."

"There must have been a lot of people you've run into over the years who have needed help. Have you camped outside their house too?"

Well, she had him there.

He sorted through his mind, then answered. "Cami's been having some problems since Mexico. She's been struggling. I don't think you know this, but one of my team members and Cami have a history, goes back since they were kids in high school. It was strong and deep. She's living with him now. Even with that kind of love and support, she still struggled and is in counseling. Nic says it's helping."

"Camilla Ross, right? I remember her. I remember what happened to her. It was...it was..." Lisa's voice trailed off.

"It *was*, baby," Raiden said as gently as he could. Again he considered his words carefully, knowing he was in landmine territory. "When those two men assaulted you both, my teammates were the ones who killed them." This time he couldn't keep his tone gentle.

"She tried to save me."

"Yes, she did."

"She put herself in danger for me. She got hurt because of me."

"No baby, she didn't. Get that clear in your mind, right now," he rumbled. "They were animals. Everything that happened was on them. They were at fault, *they* were the enemy. They did the crime. In no way shape or form are you to blame for any of it."

"But—"

"No buts. They were going to harm as many of you as possible. It was going to happen that night, rest assured. They were monsters and needed to die."

Raiden listened hard to see if Lisa had any more to say. Instead, he heard what sounded like crying. God he wanted to hold her, he wanted to tell her he had her and would keep her safe.

"So, you asked me a question, do you remember?"

He gave it a minute, and she finally responded.

"What question?"

"You asked why I was here. I'll tell you. Cami has been trying to get ahold of you. She's been worried about you. Nic called me."

"Nic, is that her high school sweetheart? The man she's living with?"

"Yep, he's a member of my SEAL team," Raiden confirmed.

"I'm confused, why did he call you?"

"You're asking a lot of hard questions today, aren't you, Lisa?"

He heard a rustle, then the blinds moved just a little. The room inside was dark; he couldn't see anything but two dainty fingers holding the blind open.

"Why you?"

"I'm the team medic. Do you remember me taking care of you?"

Again, he was met by silence, but he waited.

"Yes," she said softly.

"While we were in Mexico, it took the longest time for me to get through to you, and that made sense. I got it. But when you finally came back to yourself, your first thought was about Cami and the students. You demanded to know how they were. I thought you were going to tear a strip out of me if I didn't give you a detailed update. Do you remember that?"

"I remember. You promised me they were okay. You promised me."

"Yep, that was me."

The blind jerked back further.

"Wait a minute. You said you'd sedate me if I gave you any more trouble."

Raiden grinned. There she was, his Lisa with the fire in her voice. All was not lost.

"Yes, I did say that. You were giving me a tough time, lady. I had no choice. I had to take care of that knife wound on your arm." There had been other things he needed to make sure of, but he wasn't going to talk about that.

"That wasn't very nice."

Was that a pout? Was she teasing him? Raiden damn near rubbed his hands with glee.

"When I run across a woman as determined as you, a

man has to use every tool in his arsenal to get the job done." Raiden lowered his voice. "I was worried about you then. Just like I am now."

She didn't say anything. Shit, had he pushed too hard?

"I'm worried too. This isn't me. But I don't know how to come out of it."

Raiden sat straight up in the chair. This was his in. "Let me help, Lisa. I can help."

Her fingers disappeared and the blinds dropped closed. "Nobody can help. I need to sleep now. Just let me sleep."

6

IT WAS THE SECOND NIGHT IN THE DESERT. RAIDEN WAS ON the lounge chair with the sleeping bag unzipped—it cooled down at night in the desert, so he'd need the warmth. After Lisa had said she needed to sleep he hadn't heard any more noise from her, so he knew she'd stayed on the sofa. He hoped she was having peaceful dreams. It worried him that she was sleeping so much; she couldn't be getting enough to eat.

He propped up the book and finished it with his flashlight, then grabbed a bag of spiced tuna and some chips and made a meal for himself. That and some Gatorade and he was set. A text popped up on his phone. He wasn't surprised to see it was from Cami. She wanted to know if he'd made any progress. Raiden stepped off the patio and walked to the back fence of Lisa's yard to make the call.

"Hi, honey, how are you doing?" Raiden asked. "Are you having fun with Carys?"

"She should be home soon. There was a car wreck, so she's putting in some extra hours in the emergency room."

"Are you calling to get an update?"

"Actually, I was wondering if you could hand the phone over to Lisa. I'd really like to talk to her, and I know that her phone is turned off."

Raiden rubbed the back of his neck. "I wish I could, Cami, but she hasn't let me into her house yet."

"I don't understand, you left three days ago."

"It's not good here. I don't think she's been outta the house in weeks and I don't know if she's eating. Her house is closed up tighter than gnat's ass. With her blinds drawn shut the way they are, I don't think any light is penetrating. I was so worried about her, I would have broken in, but her air conditioning was going."

"Oh my God. Didn't you call the police so they could break in and do a welfare check?"

"Hold on a second. I've talked to her."

"Oh thank God, you had my heart racing. I was imagining all kinds of things."

"I'm sorry, honey, I should have led with that."

"So what did she have to say?"

"Mainly she wants to know why I'm here, and why I care about her wellbeing." Raiden decided not to tell Cami how out of it Lisa had sounded on the first day, and instead focus on the Lisa of today.

"So are you getting somewhere? Do you think you can get her to call me?"

"First I have to get her to open the door."

"When will that be?"

"I'm really hoping tomorrow."

"Is there anything I can do?" Cami asked.

"I'll let you know," Raiden said, ready to hang up.

"Raiden?" Cami asked tentatively.

"What, honey?"

"Why *are* you there? Why *do* you care?"

He paused, wondering if he wanted to answer the question. He really didn't know Camilla all that well, but then again, she'd been through the fire.

"I don't know how it was between you and Nic, at least not in the beginning," Raiden started. "But Lisa made an impression in Mexico. I saw her bravery, her heart, her compassion, and her grit, all of it, everything about her, and it just called to me."

"Why did you wait so long to go and see her?" Cami asked softly.

"My bad, I was planning to give it a little more time. Actually, I was watching you, seeing how long it took for you to put things behind you, then I thought I'd take my shot. I figured she'd be with Paula. I had no fucking clue that she was by herself."

And he'd regret this to his dying day.

"Are you beating yourself up?" Cami asked.

Raiden stopped short and pulled the phone away from his ear to look at it. "Maybe," he answered. Nic's Cami had a hell of a lot more wisdom than he realized.

"Well stop. You can't change the past, you can only move forward."

"I should have kept in touch with Paula. I knew that Lisa didn't have close friends, and she didn't have any family. I knew Paula was it."

Raiden put his hand on Lisa's back fence and looked up into the star-filled sky. He thought about his crazy-assed family and all the love that poured forth. He knew he was blessed. He'd even wondered if that was part of the reason that Lisa called to him so deeply, that he felt her level of isolation and wanted to enfold her into a different world.

"Don't blame yourself, Raiden. You're there, you're going to help. I know it."

Raiden couldn't even summon up a smile.

"But I have a question; are you absolutely sure you want to get this involved? This is big, and if she gets too attached and you just go away, it will be another blow. Are you up for this?"

Damn, Nic had chosen a good one.

"Cami, the woman I met in Mexico, the woman I stayed with in Miami, she tore me up. Somehow I connected with her on a cellular level. I'm thirty-three years old, and I've been around the block a few times—trust me, this has never happened to me before. I'm going to stick."

"That's good," Cami said softly. "How long are you staying?"

"As long as it takes."

IT WAS HOT, and her face was pressed against the cream-colored fabric of her sofa. Why? She turned her body and almost fell off the cushions. She thrust off the blankets and groaned as she stretched her sore muscles. Why did it feel like a sauna in here?

God, she was so thirsty. The kitchen looked like it was a million miles away, but she desperately needed some water. She threw back the blanket and stepped around the dishes on the floor in front of the coffee table.

When she looked, she couldn't find any clean glasses in the cupboards, which wasn't a surprise considering how many dirty dishes were in the sink and on the counter. She spied the dishwasher. *Maybe... Maybe...*

She opened the dishwasher and found a clean glass. She snagged it, then went to the fridge and dispensed some cold water into the glass. She greedily drank down the entire contents and went back for seconds. She opened the fridge and saw that there were some tapioca cups, and when she checked the dates, they were still good. At least she thought they were. Grabbing a clean spoon from the dishwasher, she took two cups out of the fridge, leaned against the counter, and started eating. When she started to shake, she just slid down to the floor, still eating.

How much longer until she felt well?

First, she needed to turn on the A/C. Why had she let it get so hot in here?

Everything started to flood back. Her shower, the peach-scented shampoo.

Raiden Sato.

Her head shot up and she looked at the patio blinds. Then she looked over at the clock on her microwave. Eleven seventeen p.m. Was he still here? Why would the super soldier—scratch that, Navy SEAL—from Miami have come to her house? Sure Camilla might have been worried, but having him come all the way to visit her made no sense.

She licked her spoon and pushed up from the floor, then went to throw the cups into the garbage under the sink and grimaced when she saw that it was overflowing with food she'd made but couldn't eat.

Her head dropped. There was no way she could go outside.

She plodded out to the living room and turned down the A/C, then curled back up on the couch and stared at the plastic bag of trash.

"Lisa, did I hear you moving in there?"

Lisa jerked her gaze away from the kitchen and focused on the blinds leading to the patio. She tucked her knees up closer to her chin.

"Lisa?"

If I ignore him, will he finally go away?

She looked at the patio door blinds and bit her lip.

Do I want him to go away?

The tap on her window made her damn near jump off the couch.

"I didn't mean to scare you."

She must have let out some kind of yell.

"Everything scares me. But that really scared me. Don't do it again, please."

"I promise, I won't. Feel like talking?"

Lisa pressed her lips together, tight.

He didn't say anything for what seemed like eternity.

"Lisa?"

"What do you want to talk about?" she asked.

"Wanna talk about the book?"

The book?

Then, as if he could read her mind, "You know, *Ender's Game,* by Orson Scott Card. I finished it tonight."

As if her brain were coated with syrup it took a long moment for Lisa to remember the book that she had left on her patio. It had seemed like years ago. She'd remembered that had been the first book in a new-to-her science fiction series that she'd been so excited to finish. It wasn't just years ago, wasn't it a century ago?

"I read a lot of science fiction fantasy, myself, not straight-up science fiction, but this is off the charts," Raiden said.

She smiled against her knees. He sounded so nice. And happy. Maybe even excited, and that was nice.

"You read fantasy?" she asked.

"Yeah, Tolkien, Donaldson. But this might start me on science fiction. That is, when I do read." He laughed.

Oh, his laugh was nice. She tried to remember if she'd

seen him when he'd laughed in either Mexico or Miami. She'd seen him smile before, and it was beautiful.

"Heinlein," Lisa said.

"Huh?"

"If you want to start reading science fiction, you need to read Robert Heinlein, he'll blow your mind," she whispered. She looked across her living room at the wall that was one large built-in bookcase. The bookcase was jammed to the gills, and her bedroom was even worse. Then there were the boxes of books in her bedroom closet, that and camping gear.

Huh, I haven't read a book since Mexico. Strange.

"I'm sorry, Lisa, I didn't hear you."

What were we talking about?

She shook her head, trying to clear it, then smiled.

"I said that if you ever want to read a book that will blow your mind, read *Stranger in a Strange Land* by Robert Heinlein."

"Thanks, I'll have to do that. Are you a big reader?"

"Not anymore," she whispered. Her lip trembled.

When did I lose myself?

"That doesn't sound right, whenever I meet someone who can give me book recommendations off the cuff like you just did, it sounds to me like they're a big reader. Me, I'm a little more into movies. Now my teammate, Leo, he's always hauling around a book."

"Is he another super soldier?" She almost corrected herself, but before she could, Raiden jumped in.

"Navy SEAL, honey," Raiden chuckled.

"Is there a difference?" She asked innocently. She knew there was; after all, there were forty million books in her house, it wasn't as if she hadn't read some books about the different branches of the military.

This time he let out a big laugh. "Yep, there's a difference."

"What?" She decided to draw this out. She might be tired, but it was kind of nice to have somebody to talk to. It'd been forever since she'd talked to someone. She was even feeling less foggy, but that might be from the tapioca she'd eaten.

"Well, a soldier is in the Army. I'm in the Navy, so I would be considered a Sailor. But I've had the training to become a SEAL."

She yawned. He was going to need to do all the talking. "What do you have to do to become a SEAL?"

"Lots of stuff. It takes a year and a half of training."

"That's huge. Did you always want to be a SEAL?" she asked.

"Not really. I went to college, I planned to be an engineer. Got a degree. Then realized that a lot of that job is being an individual contributor. Coming from a large extended family like I do, that's not really for me. I like being around others, working together on things, having each other's back. One of my classmates joined the Navy, and he was on leave. The way he explained how things operated, I realized that was just the place I needed to be. It wasn't long before I found out about the SEALs. That was one step further into the kind of team I wanted to belong to. It was an easy step to decide to take."

"But I heard the training is brutal."

"Well it isn't exactly a walk in the park, that's for sure. But if you have a goal, it's worth it. Anyway, what about you? I know that you worked for Wilderness Trekkers up in Alaska—talk about a job that isn't a walk in the park. What was it that Paula said, you were on the Juneau Alaska

Mountain rescue crew? I'm not thinking that was for the faint of heart, how'd that come about?"

Lisa looked at the picture of the glacier on her wall and felt a deep sense of longing. Would she ever see Alaska again?

"Lisa?"

"I got recruited," she whispered.

"Recruited? How do you get recruited to be a guide? Did you live up in Alaska?"

Lisa smiled against her knees. "Hardly. I grew up here in Tempe. But I got my first job at a dude ranch not far from here. I was the lowest of the low; I got to muck out stables. Do you know what that means?"

"I'm pretty sure that means shoveling shit."

"You got it in one."

"So Wilderness Trekkers recruited you for your shoveling shit abilities?"

She could hear the humor in his voice. Was he wearing one of his nice smiles? It made her almost want to push back the blinds again to find out.

"Not exactly. I worked at the dude ranch for two years. Turned out I was pretty good at riding horses and working with guests. Soon they were having me go along on tours. Then I got the bug to do some white river rafting over in Tucson, and ended up acting as a tour guide there."

Lisa had to haul in a deep breath. That was the most she had said in almost two months. She pushed her hands to her cheeks; they were hot. Why was she telling Raiden all of this?

"And then what?" he asked.

"It's a long story."

"But I want to hear more."

"Maybe later," she sighed. She slipped down farther on the arm of the couch. "What time is it?"

"After nine in the evening," he answered.

"All I ever do is sleep."

It was true. She'd barely eaten since getting home, and it showed. She had no idea how much weight she'd lost. At least she'd showered. She looked around her house again and thought about going back into her bedroom and locking the door, but she didn't feel like it. For some reason, it felt safer here on the couch beside Raiden.

"You know that sleeping too much is a sign of depression," Raiden said kindly.

Lisa jerked when she heard the snort come out of her nose. "Really?" she said sarcastically.

"Oh, so you do realize you're depressed."

Her back began to tense—she really didn't want to have this discussion. Really, really, really didn't want to talk about this. But at the same time, this man had flown from Miami to sleep outside her house. He was a nice man trying to help her.

This time she leaned her head against the back of her cream-colored sofa, trying to loosen up the tight muscles of her neck.

"I told you, Lisa, I just want to be here for you. I've messed up and haven't been there for others in need; I'm not going to mess up with you."

His voice sounded determined.

"I know I've asked you a hundred million times, but why me?"

"You're special. Honest to fucking God, you are one of life's special people, and I cannot stand the idea of not being here for you."

Her heart lurched. Nobody, not ever, had said she was special. Not *ever*.

"I'm in trouble," she whispered softly.

"I know," he whispered just loudly enough for her to hear. "But I'm here now, and I'm not going anywhere. I'm going to be here for you. We're going to get through this together, you get me?"

Tears welled for the thousandth time that day, but this time she managed to control them.

"I get you."

"Good, honey."

"Will you stay here with me so I can be safe?"

"Absolutely, Lisa. I'll be right here."

Her eyes drifted shut. "Thank you, Raiden."

7

Dawn in the Arizona desert was beautiful. Raiden hadn't gotten much sleep, but then he didn't need much. He'd intended to go back to the motel for a shower and the facilities, but after promising Lisa that he'd stay, he managed with a camp bath and digging a hole in the corner of her backyard.

Then, away from the house so Lisa couldn't hear, he called Kane for some intel.

"Yo, Raiden, you making any progress?" Kane asked.

"It's only been two days, so not much."

"I expected better out of you."

"This is a special case. Gotta take things slow and easy."

There was a bit of silence while Kane digested Raiden's words.

"I can see that," Kane relented.

"So did you get me the info I asked for? She's holed up and not working. How are her bills getting paid? Why in the hell did she leave a good-paying job in Alaska for a tourist guide job in Mexico? Why a house in Arizona? Inquiring minds want to know."

All of that shit had been swirling around in his head since he'd hopped the plane. He'd intended to ask Paula some of this, but she'd been unreachable, so he'd put Kane on the trail.

"Calm down, Raiden. I've got most of that figured out. She only had one relative that I could find. Weird thing is, Lisa only lived with her until she was sixteen, but anyway, the woman died without a will, so everything went to Lisa. The house was a hovel, been there forever, but it was in a neighborhood that was up and coming so it went for a whack. Lisa was set up. Not that she wasn't already doing damn well; she was being paid top dollar as a guide in Wyoming, Alaska, and the Olympic Peninsula. So her house is paid for free and clear, all of her bills are coming straight out of her checking—which is substantial—and I haven't the slightest clue why she quit all of that to head on down to Mexico."

"Why Arizona?" Raiden asked. "If all of her Wilderness jobs took her to Washington, Alaska, and Wyoming, why does she own a home in Arizona?"

"It's where she grew up. She got the money from grandma three years ago, so she could have bought in Alaska, but she didn't. The only thing I know that really keeps her here in Arizona is that she makes good-sized donations to a charity in Tempe that is dedicated to helping foster kids when they're in crisis. I haven't done any digging except for her financials, but they do depend on a lot of volunteers. My guess is she's heavily into the volunteering. My further guess would be that she has some kind of connection going back in time with someone at this charity, just haven't found it yet."

Raiden nodded. Made sense.

"That it?" Raiden asked.

"Hey, for a non-paying job, I think that's a lot."

"Tell A.J. I'll give her some Tim Tams and Twinkies for what you've accomplished."

"How does that benefit me?" Kane demanded to know.

"If you're the one giving her the treats, she'll end up being grateful to you," Raiden pointed out.

Kane chuckled. "I can make that work to my advantage. Okay, I'll dig deeper, I'll keep you posted. On to something else."

"What," Raiden asked.

"Your nephew."

"That'd be Leif, right? He's my cousin."

"Whatever. The persistent little shit." Raiden grinned, he so wasn't surprised.

"What have you got?"

"Man, as soon as I shut his shit down, he was back to it using a Mac this time, on another I.P. address. If it weren't for the fact that I was checking all of the contacts on his original account, I probably wouldn't have found him."

"Sure would have sucked if you had been outmaneuvered by a little shit," Raiden snorted.

"Fuck you, Sato."

"So, did you shut him down again?" Raiden asked.

"Kind of got sick of his games. Did one better. I figured it was time to put paid to his business altogether. Put a stall on all of his communications. It gave me time to reproduce his test answers but change them around. They're now wrong. Just did it with three of his customers. The others, I just stopped them from getting their incoming, so they were out their cash."

Raiden grinned. "So he's stolen money, plus given out crap to people. Oh, this is not going to go over well."

"You got it."

"I'll give it a day, then give him a call." Raiden imagined what Leif would be thinking then.

"Hopefully this lesson will get through," Kane said.

"To tell you the truth, I'm not sure it will," Raiden sighed. "But one can hope."

"Yep. Well, good luck with both projects, I've got to go."

Raiden could hear the grin in his friend's voice, as he hung up.

LISA WOKE up and stretched and something felt different. She was on her couch. She tried to think about what was wrong but came up with nothing. Her eyes hit the front door. Locks were in place. Then the back door, locks were good there. She grimaced when she saw the trash bag. She sat up higher on the couch and threw her legs down so she was sitting up, careful not to step on any of the dirty dishes.

What was wrong? She bent down and picked up the plateful of congealed spaghetti that was close to her right foot, and set it on the coffee table.

What was wrong?

Then she remembered.

Raiden.

Raiden was outside, and he was making sure she was safe. She was finally safe. Nobody was going to come inside and get her. She rolled her shoulder muscles, they felt good. Not hard, not tense, they felt like she'd had a good night's sleep. Even her lower back felt good, even though she'd slept on the sofa.

"Raiden?" She called out softly.

"Yeah? I was hoping you'd wake up soon. It's good to hear your voice."

That hit her right in her solar plexus. So weird that he would like to hear her voice. But then again, she was really glad to hear his voice too.

"What time is it?" she asked.

"Eight o'clock in the morning," he answered. "You missed a beautiful sunrise."

Lisa closed her eyes for just a moment and pictured an Arizona sunrise. They were one of the best things about living in a desert, that and sunsets. Her eyes shot open and she grinned when she realized that she'd actually pictured a sunrise instead of some kind of nightmare.

"I like sunrises."

"So do I. So what can I get you for breakfast?" Raiden asked. "How does an Egg McMuffin sound?"

Lisa felt her stomach rumble. She placed her hand over her stomach and realized she didn't feel queasy. Actually, that sounded good, but then her head swiveled to her front door. She saw the pizza pan resting against it and the deadbolts. She couldn't let him in.

"I could leave it at your door, and you could just pick it up off your porch after I've left," he whispered. It was as if he read her mind.

"I'm not really hungry," she demurred.

"Do you have enough food in there?" Raiden asked.

Lisa did a sweep of her house. Once again her eyes lighted on the grocery bags on her dining room table. How old were those now? Three days? A week?

"I'm fine for food," she assured Raiden.

"Are you cooking for yourself?" he asked.

"That doesn't matter. Look, I don't want to talk about it, okay?"

She could hear his sigh through the glass door, and she knew he wanted her to talk because he sighed loudly.

"Can we talk about something else?" Lisa realized it was nice to talk to somebody. Her stomach growled again. She'd only eaten some crackers and tapioca, washed down with Sprite. She really was hungry now that she was keeping food down. Finally. What else was there to eat?

"Sure, Lisa, what would you like to talk about?"

"World peace?"

Raiden let out a long laugh. "We're going to be here for a while."

"I don't have any plans at the moment, do you?" she asked.

"I was thinking about getting an Egg McMuffin."

Her stomach rumbled again. She was feeling better than yesterday. Less shaky. She got up and went to the dining room table and looked into the bags of groceries, ignoring the noxious odors. Thank God she hadn't ordered milk or eggs. The only real perishable items were the peaches, cherries, and yogurt. The yogurt was bulging but hadn't exploded yet, so that was a blessing. The bananas were brown, but the bread still looked edible. There were some boxes of macaroni and cheese, but there was no way she was going to boil water and she didn't have any milk.

"Lisa?" Raiden called out.

She wandered back to the couch and sat down.

"I'd like a bacon, egg, and cheese biscuit," she said.

"Hash browns?" Raiden immediately asked.

The thought of all that grease made her grimace. "No. But can you get me some milk? A lot of milk?"

"Sure, honey. I could go to the grocery store too. Is there anything else you want?"

"No, just that."

"I'll be back as soon as I can. I'm leaving right now. Are you going to be okay with me gone?"

Lisa did a gut check. It was morning, not night.

"Yeah, I'll be fine."

8

RAIDEN'S PALMS WERE ACTUALLY FUCKING SWEATY. WHEN THE hell was the last time that had happened? And all because he was going through the McDonald's drive-thru. At long last, he was making some headway. Some significant headway. Wasn't he?

Raiden shook his head after he took his food. For fuck's sake he was thinking like a thirteen-year-old girl. He rolled down the windows on the way back to Lisa's house and turned up the music. By the time he rolled up the drive, he was feeling like himself.

He put three bags on the front porch, one with her breakfast sandwich, one with five cartons of cold milk, and one with cinnamon rolls and apple pies, hoping that the treats would tempt her. He hopped the fence with his goods and was immediately at her sliding glass door.

"Lisa?"

"Yeah?"

"Your food is at the front door."

"At the front?"

Her voice sounded wrong when she asked the question.

"Yeah, honey, shouldn't I have put it there? That's where you've gotten your groceries, right?"

She didn't answer.

"I don't want to open my front door," she said when she finally spoke.

He rested his forehead against the glass of her patio door. She sounded so sad.

"Are you scared to?"

"I think so. I don't know anymore. I'm less scared with you here. So maybe it's not that. Maybe it's getting to be a habit. I'm not sure." The last almost sounded like a question.

"Honey, since you've been in your house, have you opened a window or a patio door?"

"No," she said hesitantly.

"Would you like to open your bedroom window just a crack and have me pass through the food?"

"No!" she said vehemently.

Well, that answered that. "Is it because you don't want me within touching distance?"

"Uhm."

Raiden waited.

"I'm not sure. Maybe."

"How about if you opened this patio door, and I wait in the backyard, not on the patio. You'll be able to see me, but I'll be far enough away that I won't be able to reach you while you pick up your food. Would that work?"

Again there was a long pause.

"Raiden, that is so pathetic that I can't even open my front door to get my food anymore. I've been afraid to order more groceries. It's been getting worse."

It sounded like she was close to tears.

"I don't know, Lisa. Seems to me since I got here, you've been doing better, don't you think?"

He saw the blinds shift, once again he saw those dainty fingers. "Maybe. I have been talking to you, that's an improvement."

"And you're considering eating a McDonald's breakfast sandwich. I think things are looking up for you."

"You could be right."

"So what do you think? Could you open the patio door and grab the bags of food?"

"Yeah," she whispered.

"Okay, give me a second and I'll go get them from the front porch. I'll let you know when they're set up so you can get them, okay?"

"Yeah."

Raiden hopped the fence and had the food back in no time. He placed the food right by the lip of the sliding glass door so she wouldn't have to open it much.

"Okay, honey, it's there." He moved backward to the edge of the patio and waited.

He saw her hands moving the safety bar at the base of the door, then he finally saw Lisa for the first time in seven weeks. He saw her hands, her body, and her face as she picked up the three bags. She stared at him for a moment like a scared rabbit, then she gave a tentative smile.

He smiled back, not wanting to say anything that might scare her.

She clutched her bounty and tugged it inside, then shut the door. Raiden felt like he had run a marathon in record time. It was wonderful. Now he was ready to push just a little bit more. Just a little.

He went back to the chair, not the chaise lounge, and sat down. He opened up his two breakfast sandwiches and placed them on their wrappers. Then he opened one of his two bottles of orange juice and got ready for his next move.

"Lisa?"

"Why did you get so much food?" she asked.

"If you don't like it, you can throw it away," he said. "But I was hoping it might tempt you. I want to take care of you."

"Oh."

She didn't say anything else, so he was ready to go for the gusto. "Lisa, I really hate eating by myself."

"Oh."

"Do you think you could open your blinds and we could have breakfast together?"

Even from where he was sitting he could hear the big breath of air she sucked in. He knew he was pushing, but he needed to. The sooner he could get her out of her house and into counseling the better off she would be.

"I don't think I can, Raiden."

"How about if you just pulled back your blinds just a little bit, maybe six inches or so, just so that I can see your beautiful eyes, how about that?"

"I... I..."

"Honey, I just want to see you while we have breakfast together. Nothing else. Nothing scary, just see you while we talk and share a meal. Is that okay?"

For the longest time, she didn't respond and Raiden was sure he'd overplayed his hand, then he saw the blinds move. He grinned as he saw them pull back almost a foot. *Thank the good Lord.*

"You really can't see me from the couch, so I have to move. Wait a minute."

"Okay, do what you have to do," Raiden encouraged.

The blinds opened a little more, then through the gloom inside the house, he saw Lisa was sitting in a dining room chair beside the open blinds. She was leaning over the breakfast sandwich in her lap and the milk carton was on the floor in front of her. Finally, she looked up at him. Then she gave him a small smile and he felt like he had won the gold at the Olympics.

"Hi, honey."

"Hi, Raiden."

"It's good to see you. I've been really worried about you."

"Can we not talk about that?"

"Sure, let's just eat our breakfast," he agreed. As he took a big bite out of his sandwich he watched her take a dainty bite out of hers. She followed it by taking a sip of milk. She didn't go for another bite, which made sense; her body probably wasn't used to food. She looked gaunt. She'd really lost weight, at least fifteen pounds since he'd seen her in Miami. He'd taken note of her back then, five foot nine, toned body but still with curves. Now even in the shapeless pajamas, he could see that she had lost those curves. What's more, her face looked too damned thin.

Lisa took another bite of her sandwich.

"Do you like your food?" he asked.

"Yeah. This has always been one of my favorites, but then I started eating huevos rancheros at the dude ranch and McDonald's breakfast started coming in second place."

Raiden made a mental note to get that for her tomorrow morning.

"Honey, with you sitting back there, I'm having a little trouble hearing you. Is there any way you might consider opening the sliding glass door just an inch?"

Her eyes shot to his. He could see the fear and he hated it.

"You don't have to if you don't want to, but I won't try to come into your house. You can trust me. I just want to be able to hear you while we have breakfast together."

She gave him a long considering look, then set down her

sandwich, got up, and inched to the door. After unlocking the door she opened it just a little. "Is this enough?" she asked.

"Yeah, Lisa, it is. I can hear you much better now."

She nodded, then backed on up toward her chair. He could tell she didn't want to turn her back on him. When she was settled he gave her a warm smile. He waited until she smiled back, then he asked his first question.

"So, Lisa, you never told me how you got from Arizona to Alaska."

"It was one of the clients here in Arizona who did a tour up in Alaska. Apparently, they had good things to say about me to Paula. She checked me out and recruited me for Wilderness Trekkers."

"That's it, huh?" Raiden was positive there was a hell of a lot more to the story than that.

"Yep, that's it." She took another bite of her sandwich. He watched as she took a long pull of her milk, then placed the carton back down on the tile floor and reached into one of the bags and pulled out another carton, and opened it.

"So how did you jump from guiding people in the deserts of Arizona to the wilds of Alaska? That sounds like a pretty big shift."

"It really was. To begin with, Paula just had me go out on the tours, do some cooking, and hand-holding with the clients. I did that for a year, at the same time I started to learn how to mountain climb. That shit was hard. It took me about four years before I got my first low-level American Mountain Guide Association certificate. In the meantime, I could take people on hikes, horseback riding, and whitewater rafting."

Raiden grinned; seemed like food was perking her up and getting her to be more talkative. Great, now he knew.

"What made you decide to work at a dude ranch when you were eighteen? Why not college?"

He watched as Lisa put down her sandwich on her lap and looked him straight in the eye. "I really didn't have much of a choice. I was in foster care from sixteen to eighteen. As soon as my eighteenth birthday arrived, I didn't have anywhere to live. Luckily, I knew it was coming, so I'd been looking for a job that provided room and board. Reever's Ranch provided it."

Raiden knew that was how the foster system worked. Once the foster kids hit eighteen the checks from the government dried up, so the foster parents closed their doors to the foster kids. There was no cushion for these kids, no nothing. Not like a birth child.

"Sounds like you did this smart."

Lisa tilted her head in a half nod. "Tried to. Anyway, Mr. and Mrs. Reever were good to me. I was damned lucky that they allowed me to learn on their ranch, and try different things and grow into different positions. Not a lot of people would be like them."

She stopped talking and picked up her sandwich. "Now you do some talking." She took a bite and nodded her head.

"What do you want me to talk about?"

Even as she chewed he saw a smile form. She picked up her milk, then washed down her bite of food. "Anything, Raiden. Talk about anything at all."

"I'm an only child, but with all of my cousins, it feels like I have a crowd of brothers and sisters. Mom's sisters and kids were always over at our house. She was the oldest sister, so our house was the gathering point. I'm the oldest cousin, so I got stuck babysitting a lot."

"Did you change diapers?"

"More than I want to remember. I have twelve younger

cousins on my mother's side and three on my father's side. The three on my father's side live in Minneapolis, but Mom's all live in Virginia Beach."

"Wait a minute, I thought you lived in Miami."

"No, I'm stationed at Little Creek near Virginia Beach, another reason I wanted to be a SEAL. I knew that you get stationed out of Virginia Beach or San Diego. I wanted to stay near family." He took a bite of his second sandwich.

"How old are you?"

"I'm thirty-three, and before you ask, never been married despite my mother's best matchmaking efforts. Actually not just my mom, my aunties have all tried too. I guess I must just have the bachelor gene. How about you, have you ever been married?"

Her body jerked and some of the milk spilled out of the carton. She shook her head. "No," she finally whispered. "Never been married."

"Close?" he asked.

"Not even close," she whispered again.

"How about—"

"I thought we were talking about you." she interrupted.

"Oh yeah. So, I come from a large family that is in everybody's business."

"Sounds nice." Her head was down as she looked at the half-eaten sandwich in her lap. Raiden kicked himself for having brought up his family, considering she had been in foster care.

"Mostly it is," he agreed. "Right now there is one cousin who is a pain in my ass."

She looked up at him again.

"Are you going to finish your breakfast?" he asked.

He watched as she yawned.

"I don't think I can. You bought too much food." Then

she yawned again.

She didn't look good. She looked far too thin, and Raiden would bet his bottom dollar that her coloring would be pasty, even with her Hispanic heritage. Even from here, he could see the deep bruises under her eyes.

She yawned yet again. "Tell me about your cousin."

"I tell you what, why don't you put the rest of the food away in your refrigerator, take a breather, and then we can talk again. How does that sound?"

Her eyes flashed up at him and he watched her consider his suggestion. "I think that would be a good idea."

"You know what else would be a good idea?"

"What?"

"Maybe tonight you might want to think about your favorite thing for dinner, and I can bring that. Then, if you're up for it, maybe, just maybe, you might invite me inside."

"No!" she practically yelled.

"Okay, okay, okay." He watched and listened as her breath heaved in and out.

"You can't come into my house. You can't."

Raiden held up his hands. "Honey, I won't come into your house. I promise. I promise. Please calm down. I won't come inside. Can you calm down?"

She gripped the arms of her chair. Even from where he was sitting he could see her knuckles turning white.

"I can't breathe," she choked out the words.

"It'll get better, I promise," he said soothingly. "Work with me, baby, take one little sip of air and hold it. Can you do that? Just one little sip." He watched as she did. "Now let it out."

She looked up at him. "Do it again, honey. One tiny breath in. Hold it. One breath out." He continued to walk her through it until her eyes didn't look so panicked.

"You okay?"

She nodded.

"So, I take it me coming inside is a no?" he teased.

She gave him a fierce glare, then sat back and sighed. "I kind of like the fact you're not treating me like an invalid," she whispered.

"That's because you're not. You've just lost your way for a little bit. This will pass."

"Ya think?"

"I know it. So if I can't come inside, how about you joining me out on the patio for dinner?"

Her eyes flashed up at him as she gave him an incredulous look. "Did you just ask that?"

"You said you liked me not treating you like spun glass, so I'm not. Think about it—dinner, under the stars, with a Navy SEAL who will keep you safe."

She stared at him for a long time. "That's a big ask."

"I know, honey. I know. But I think you're ready for that. I think it's time. What's your favorite food?"

She wrapped up her sandwich and put it into one of the bags.

"What kind of food do you like for dinner?" he asked again.

She sighed. "Italian."

"What is your favorite dish?"

"Eggplant parmesan."

"I'll pick that up tonight. In the meantime, why don't you put your food in the fridge, and take some time to yourself? Read a book, or get some sleep. How does that sound?"

"Yeah, I'll put this in the fridge," she agreed.

He watched as she gathered everything up, then shut the door and closed the blinds. He prayed that he hadn't pushed too hard.

9

CURLING UP IN THE CLEAN SHEETS AND COMFORTER IN THE guest bedroom felt good, real good. She hadn't wanted to sleep here before because there were no locks on the door, but with Raiden outside, she felt safe enough to do so. The temperature in the house was finally right, too. Not too cold and not too hot, just comfortable.

She was tired, but she had too many thoughts whirling around in her head to go to sleep, so she'd grabbed a couple of books off her bookshelf to re-read. Because Raiden had mentioned fantasy, she'd plucked a book by Stephen R. Donaldson off her shelf and dove into that. It kind of fit her mood. All about a man who woke up in a strange world and didn't fit in.

"No!"

"Stop!"

"Please, Damon, stop!"

She tried to fight, but she couldn't get him off her. No

matter how hard she tried she couldn't get away. He wouldn't listen to her.

"No! Please, don't hurt me!"

Lisa heard pounding. A voice that wasn't Damon's was shouting her name. "Lisa, answer me! I'm coming in if you don't answer me. Can you hear me?"

She looked at the lamp beside the bed and realized the pounding was on the window and the voice was Raiden's. It had been a bad dream.

"I'm coming in."

"No!"

"Okay, you haven't answered me, so I'm coming in." Raiden's voice sounded almost frantic.

"No! Don't come in, Raiden!" She didn't want him to see her like this. She didn't want him to see her house like this. She would die if he saw what she'd been reduced to. "Please, don't come in."

"What's wrong, baby? Talk to me."

"It was a bad dream."

"Come to the patio door. Let me see you. Come talk to me."

"It was nothing. Just a bad dream." How come Damon was still stealing her life away after all these years? Almost ten years later and he still was wrenching bits and pieces of her apart, leaving her with nothing. She'd never even been with a man; she couldn't trust them after Damon.

"It wasn't nothing. God, Lisa, let me help you."

Now it sounded like it was wrenching Raiden apart. How was that possible?

She dropped her head into her hands. Years. Years and years and years she had gone without having nightmares about Damon, but since Mexico, the dreams had come back, and they were mixed up with her hanging by her wrists in the jungle, that animal putting his hands on her, pawing at her, his hands on her breasts, bruising her, his hands down her pants. Everything was all mixed up. Everything was a nightmare. One that made her stop caring for herself.

"Lisa, will you come to the patio door?"

"No. It's no use."

"Will you let me in?"

"No!" She heard herself; her voice was panicked and strident. She sounded like a shrew.

"It's okay, baby, I won't come in then. But you scared the fuck out of me. Please come to the door and let me see you. Please, I'm begging you."

She looked over at the open door to the bedroom. The door that could only be open because Raiden was there to protect her.

"Okay."

She lurched out of bed, the book falling to the floor. She was wearing thin cotton pajama shorts and a tank top. She thought about changing but it was too much effort. She flashed back to the Mexican jungle and remembered Raiden caring for her, tending her scratches and bruises along with the knife wound. He'd seen a lot of her that night. Seen a lot and had not taken advantage of her.

She trudged to the sliding glass door in the living room and pushed back the blinds. God bless him, he wasn't right there next to the glass where he would overwhelm her; he was a few feet away, his expression concerned.

"See, I'm all right."

"You look like you've seen a ghost."

She let out a short, anguished laugh. "Yeah, you could say that."

"Who's Damon?"

Fuck, had she'd said his name during her sleep?

"Nobody."

"He sure sounded like somebody. You sounded scared of him," he said softly.

"He's nobody," she insisted. She saw Raiden's face. He knew she was lying. "Please, just drop it. Please?"

He nodded.

She looked past him and noticed that the sky was purple. It was sunset. "I haven't seen that in a while."

"What, baby?"

"A desert sunset."

He looked over his shoulder, then turned back to her and smiled. "It's beautiful. Almost as beautiful as you are."

Those words made her sad. She knew they weren't true. Maybe once she'd been beautiful, but that was a long time ago. She reached for the blinds.

"Wait!"

"What?"

"Did you think about dinner? I have an order in. Will you eat out here with me?" He walked two steps forward and placed his hand on the glass. "Will you?"

She looked at his big hand, then into his warm brown eyes. Safe, he made her feel safe.

"I don't think I can."

"I've gotta ask. It's important. Will you give me an honest answer?"

His eyes were so warm. So sincere. He was actually here, and had been for almost three days. Lisa still wasn't sure why he cared so much.

"I'll be honest."

"Do you like feeling the way you do?"

His question reverberated around her head like a tornado. It spun around for a long time before it finally rested and she could focus.

"I hate it. I hate feeling like I do, but I don't know how to stop," she whispered.

"Cami made it stop."

"Camilla?"

"Yes, Camilla. She made it stop. I can't make it stop for you—not entirely—but I can put you on the right path. Will you let me do that?"

The tornado started up again, but Lisa shook her head, willing it to settle.

"How?"

"Little by little, hour by hour. We started this morning with breakfast. We'll continue with dinner tonight."

"But not inside, right?" Her stomach heaved at the idea of him coming into her house.

"I promise, not inside."

"Okay."

"Close the blinds baby, I'll be back with food as fast as I can. It's chilly out here, so dress warmly, okay?"

She nodded.

EARLIER, Raiden had texted Max. He'd been hoping that he could hear from him to see how things were going. Supposedly this was going to be an easy op, but Raiden wouldn't be surprised if his boss had been blowing smoke up his ass just to make him feel better about taking leave. Things couldn't have worked out better when he got a call back as he was making his way to the restaurant to pick up the Italian food.

"How's everything going?" Max asked.

"That's my question," Raiden responded as he pulled onto the highway.

"Something tells me that out of the two of us, I have the easier job."

"Tell you what, you give me the low-down first, then it'll be my turn." Raiden waited to see what Max would say to his deal.

"Sounds good. Can't give you all the specifics, but suffice it to say, we're in the desert and Cullen is being a smartass, Kane has gotten us the info we need, and in three days we should have a bead on the targets." That explained why Kane could still work on things for Raiden.

"So right now you're just kickin' back?"

"I wish. We've been having to do some on-the-ground training with some newbies. Not a lot to work with, but we're trying."

Raiden chuckled. They'd been through that drill many times before.

"So if Cullen is busy being a smartass did you make him point for training?"

"Oh yeah, he's definitely heading things up, it's only fair. But, like always, Zed's working with the youngest among the group we're supposed to train and he's already on his way to sortin' their shit out."

"In three days?"

"What can I say, Zed is Zed."

Raiden laughed. That was true.

"And you?"

"I'm working with their leader. He's stuck in his ways, he doesn't think he needs us. He needs to go. His second-in-command is a good guy, so I'll be making a recommendation that he be put in charge."

That was how it worked; if you were in the field you didn't have much time to figure things out—you had to get shit sorted fast and move on down the road, otherwise, people got hurt.

"Now your turn, how's it going?" Max asked.

"She spiraled into agoraphobia."

Max was silent. "Raiden," Max started slowly. "Based on who she is, her job and everything, I'm surprised that one incident sent her that far off the rails. After all, the woman I saw in Mexico was such a goddamn fighter."

Raiden had thought the same damn thing. He in no way, shape, or form wanted to belittle the trauma Lisa had suffered at the hands of the animals in Mexico. God knew that could knock a lot of people, man or woman, into a hell of a spiral, but this had taken him by surprise.

Until he had heard her dream about Damon.

"Max, I'm not going to get into any of Lisa's personal business with you, okay?"

"Sure. I wouldn't want you to," Max replied immediately.

"But I'm not sure this is the first trauma she's gone through."

"Ah fuck," Max breathed out. "Fuck, fuck, fuck."

"Exactly."

"Goddammit, Raiden. What in the hell can I do to help?"

Raiden turned on his blinker and pulled into the Italian restaurant's parking lot.

"If I think of anything, I'll let you know."

For the longest time, there was silence on the line, so long that Raiden thought the call had been dropped.

"Max, you there?"

"Yeah, I'm here. Can I say something?"

"Shoot."

"I've got to say, with all this swirling around this woman, she couldn't be in better hands."

Ah hell.

"Gotta go, Max. You stay safe, you hear?"

"Always." He could hear the grin in his Lieutenant's voice.

"Bye."

"Bye."

LISA PULLED the cardigan tight around her body against the fresh, cool evening air and looked at the food in front of her. Raiden hadn't left it in a Styrofoam container—he'd put it on a paper plate and had plenty of napkins, and four different beverages available for her along with a cup to use. Then there was the camp lantern. The man had gone all-out.

"You doing okay?"

She nodded and pulled the sweater even tighter as she sat on the edge of the chair. Raiden was relaxed as he sat lower on the side of the lounge chair.

"This is more than I ordered."

"They had a hell of a menu, so I couldn't resist. You should see what's for dessert."

Lisa's eyes shot to his. "Dessert? Raiden, breakfast this morning is the most I've eaten in one day in weeks."

"Honey, just eat what you can, and put the rest away for tomorrow. But I want to tell you, there is tiramisu and chocolate layer cake for dessert, your choice, so you might want to go easy on the eggplant."

"Chocolate layer cake?" She didn't know if her stomach would revolt or savor that treat. She picked up a fork and noticed that even her fingers looked thin. Goddammit, she sure should try to eat a little of everything.

"Oh, before you cut into your eggplant, I forgot the soft

breadsticks." Raiden rummaged through the big bag and pulled out a smaller bag. He placed one breadstick on her plate and three on his. Her mouth watered.

Lisa put down her fork, let go of her sweater, and broke apart the breadstick so she could dip it into the marinara sauce, and took a bite.

"This is wonderful," she said after she swallowed.

He smiled, huge.

"Glad you like it. Now, what beverage can I pour you from the selection?"

She looked over all of the bottles and pointed to the lemonade. He poured and she took a sip of her drink, then took another bite of marinara-coated breadstick and grinned. She looked around her patio and enjoyed the cool air floating around her.

"This is nice. It's not as scary as I thought. The last time I've been in the backyard was when I installed the padlock."

"Yeah, I noticed that. When did you do that?"

"I ordered it online and installed it a week and a half ago. It was right after the sheriff came and did a perimeter check."

"Perimeter check? Were you in the military? That sounds official," he frowned.

"That's what the deputy called it."

"Why did you call the sheriff?"

"I called nine-one-one, and they sent the sheriff. I was sure someone was outside. It was the second time I had heard someone."

"What did the sheriff say?"

"They noticed that the dirt was disturbed, but they said that it could have been some kind of animal because they didn't see any human footprints. I didn't let them into the house, and I know what I was acting like, so they probably thought I was some kind of crazy lady. What's more, this wasn't the first call."

"It wasn't?"

"I called once after I got home from Mexico."

"When was that, honey?"

"I really can't remember exactly, dates have gotten away from me. Do you know that I just realized it was December?"

"I don't need a date—can you remember if it was in the first or second week when you got home?"

"It was almost immediately after Paula brought me home." She looked up at him, her eyes shining brightly. "I was a mess." Then she huffed out a laugh. "What am I talking about, I'm still a mess, aren't I?"

"Stop it," he chided softly. "Be nice to my friend."

"So it was about ten days ago that you called in the last time?"

She nodded.

"Did they find anything the first time? Anything disturbed?"

She shook her head.

"Okay. Well, you did the right thing installing the padlock."

"It scared the crap out of me going outside," she admitted.

"But you did, and that's pretty impressive. Now you better dig into your eggplant before it gets cold."

———

HE WATCHED as she went back inside. It had been a great meal. She hadn't eaten a lot, but he'd bet his bottom dollar she'd consumed more calories today than she had in the last week. Raiden picked up the rest of the trash from the meal, then hopped the fence and went to the garbage bins under her carport and saw that they were overflowing.

"Ah, shit."

He looked out into the cul-de-sac. Nope, nobody had their trash bins sitting out by the sidewalk, so tomorrow wasn't a pick-up. But what was worse, he couldn't imagine how much trash she probably had accumulated inside her house. Was that part of the reason she didn't want him inside?

He thought back to her vehemence and wondered if it might have been hiding shame.

"Shit, shit, shit."

He looked back at her house with a pang of regret. Why hadn't he thought to check on her sooner? Why had it taken Cami to call his attention to this?

He walked slowly back to the fence, berating himself the entire way. Great, he wanted to give her time, but he should have fucking known better. He should have fucking *known* better. At the very least, he should have called Paula.

He hopped the fence and looked at the little tableau on the patio. It had been a nice dinner, but it wasn't enough. She needed more help than just him tempting her out of her house. It was time for some big guns. He took out his phone and sent a text, knowing it was too late on the East coast for a phone call. He'd wait until morning for a discussion. In the meantime, he knew he wouldn't get any sleep. He turned the lounge chair around so it was facing the house, then he snagged his sleeping bag from where it was sitting near the pergola post, rolled it out on top of the chaise, and settled down. He could see a light in a different bedroom than the master, shining through the blinds. Lisa must be in the guest room.

God, he hoped she wouldn't have another nightmare. Who in the hell was Damon, and where in the hell was he, because wherever the fuck he was, Raiden wanted to get his hands on him.

He moved the lounge chair closer to the guest bedroom so he would hear any sound that Lisa might make during the night, then he teed up his phone and downloaded the next book in the *Ender* series. It was going to be a long night, so he might as well keep himself entertained.

10

RAIDEN'S PHONE VIBRATED FIRST THING. HE'D BEEN USING Lisa's outside electrical socket to keep it charged.

"Hey, Cami, thanks for calling."

"Raiden, I'm so glad you called. I've appreciated the texts, but I was really hoping to talk to you. How is Lisa doing? How are you doing?"

Raiden smiled. And wasn't that just the wonder of Camilla Ross? Not only was she worried about Lisa Garcia, but she was worried about how the situation might be affecting him. Nic had tied himself to a good woman.

"I'm doing fine, but Lisa is not doing well. She's been holed up in her house for the last seven weeks. She's gotten some groceries off her porch and went into her backyard once, but that's been it. All of her blinds are shut, and she won't let anybody inside. She's lost a lot of weight that she couldn't afford to lose."

"If she's not coming out, and nobody's coming in, how do you know she's lost weight?" Cami asked.

"We had breakfast together and she opened her sliding

glass door a bit to sit with me. Then she came out on her patio last night to eat some Italian food."

"Go Team Raiden," Cami whispered.

Raiden smiled again.

"But it's not enough, Cami. She's having bad dreams. She's terrified of me seeing the inside of her house. I'm worried it's a mess and she's embarrassed."

"That shouldn't matter," Cami objected.

"Exactly. It's just part of her depression. But she doesn't see it like that."

There was a long pause. "She wouldn't."

"Cami—"

"I can come out there."

"That would be too much. She's got to ask."

"I hate that. I just want to come out there. Do you know what she did for all of us? Do you know how damn much she did?" She sounded so fierce. "Raiden, I want to be there for her, ya' know?"

"I know, sweetie, I know. I'm going to try to get her to talk to you today. It'll come from my cell; be ready for it, okay?"

"Absolutely."

"You doing okay? This is the first time Nic's gone on a mission."

"Hell yeah, I'm doing okay. I'm a SEAL's woman. I was born for this."

Raiden grinned. He didn't quite believe her, but he grinned. "Camilla, that wasn't quite what I meant. Lisa isn't the only one who went through hell seven weeks ago. I know damn well you were brave and fierce and protected those kids. But you had a trauma too. So how are *you* doing?"

Her voice went soft. "Nic's been taking care of me. He made me come stay with Carys. I've landed gentle."

"Cami—"

"Now I want to be there for Lisa. You arrange the call, and I'll be waiting. Got it?"

"I got it, Cami." He hung up, shaking his head. *Yep, Nic got a good one.*

Now it was time to get some exercise. What he really wanted was a run around the neighborhood. Just twenty miles, was that asking for too much? But it was. He needed to stay here. So time for some physical training. He went to work.

Crunches.

Push-ups.

Squats.

Planks.

Lunges.

After three hours he was really feeling it. He hosed off and changed clothes. Then he noticed a light come on in the house. Not a soft light like a bed lamp, but an overhead light. It was in the master bedroom. Maybe Lisa was taking a shower.

LISA BLINKED BACK tears as she looked around the master bathroom, then she slowly turned and saw the state of her bedroom. She should have never turned on the overhead light. Even from the bathroom door, she could see some of the shards of glass from where her lamp had crashed to the floor. Clothes were strewn everywhere; so were open bags of chips and cookies that had to be weeks old, because she couldn't remember how long it had been since she could choke down cookies or chips.

Just like in her living room she saw dishes, only they

were upside down because they'd spilled over, so there was dried oatmeal on the floor. She covered her eyes as her back hit the doorjamb and she slowly slid down until her ass hit the floor. Quiet sobs wracked her body. She did everything in her power not to make any noise, not wanting Raiden to hear her. She would die if he heard her and wanted to come inside.

She didn't know how long she stayed there. It really didn't matter. What mattered was that she needed to figure out a way to get Raiden to leave. She had to make him leave. She tried to stand up, but she couldn't, not even using the doorjamb as leverage. She couldn't get up; her legs just wouldn't work.

How was she going to make Raiden leave if she couldn't even get up off the floor?

A trickle of cold air hit the back of her neck—the air conditioner kicking in. For just a second, one brief moment, it felt like she was back in Alaska. God, wouldn't that be a dream? Back in Alaska, before she'd ever thought of going to Mexico, before another bad dream slammed into old nightmares, causing her to go crazy.

Lisa took a deep breath and pulled her head up off her knees and tried getting up again. This time she managed to get to her feet. Ignoring the mess, she hit the switch on the overhead light and shambled out. She veered to the guest bedroom; at least it wasn't as dirty.

"I have to get rid of Raiden," she murmured as she shuffled toward the clean bed. At that thought her gut clenched. If he left, she wouldn't be safe. She'd have to lock herself back up in her bedroom again. Her hands balled up into fists and she took a swing against the bedroom wall.

"Lisa! What's going on in there?"

Dammit!

She took another swing, not caring that her knuckles hurt.

"Answer me. What are you doing?"

He sounded like he was inside her bedroom. She swung her head around, then ran to the window and slammed her palms against the blinds. "Don't come inside!" she screamed. "It's none of your fucking business what I do! Get the hell out of here! Leave me the fuck alone!" She kept pounding on the blinds, over and over again. She let out a shriek when the right side came undone and crashed down onto the windowsill, letting in daylight, exposing her, forcing her to see Raiden's caring and compassionate face.

Her palms smeared down the bare window, slowly sliding downwards as she stared at the man that she so desperately needed, but who scared the hell out of her. He needed to get gone.

"Please leave," she whispered. "If you care about me, please leave."

She wanted to turn around and run out of the room, but her eyes couldn't look away from his—they were stuck. Somehow he was controlling her just with his eyes, forcing her to stay with him.

Then it got worse, because he spoke.

"Lisa, I'm going to stay with you. Remember, I care about you. I care so much about you, and I'm not leaving you. I'm going to help you. I promise you."

Her hands kept slipping until her fingertips gripped the edge of the windowsill. "I'm broken, you can't help," she whispered.

"Cami was broken too," he whispered back. "Remember? They broke her too."

Snippets of her being tied up in the jungle. Camilla was on the other end, she was being touched too. Brutalized.

"Do you remember how they hurt Cami?" Raiden asked. Lisa nodded.

"She wants to talk to you."

Lisa shook her head. "I don't want her here."

"On the phone, baby, just on the phone," he said gently. "Will you take my phone so she can talk to you?"

Through the window, Lisa could see Raiden holding up his cell phone. Even as scared as she was, she could see that he was calm. Lisa latched onto his calm. She took a breath. And another.

"Is Camilla all right?"

"She is, honey. She's been surrounded by people who love her, and she's been talking to someone who's been helping. She wants to talk to you. She wants to help."

Acid churned in her stomach. The idea of letting Camilla down hurt. She knew that she would want to help, but there was no helping her.

"Lisa, tell me what you're thinking," Raiden coaxed.

Lisa shook her head, her dark hair got into her eyes and now she couldn't see Raiden anymore. Maybe that was for the best.

"Lisa, please talk to me. What are you thinking?"

"What if Camilla can't help me and she gets mad at me?"

"Ah, honey, she won't get mad at you. She cares about you like I do, she wants to help. Would you get mad at Cami if she was hurting?"

Lisa rolled his question around in her head. She remembered Camilla's whimpers in the Mexican jungle. There was no way she could ever be mad at Camilla.

She lifted one of her hands off the windowsill and pushed back her hair. "All right, I'll talk to her."

Raiden's eyes burned bright as he smiled. "Can you open the window so I can give you the phone?"

She looked behind her and sighed with relief when she realized the guest bedroom was not like the other rooms in her house. She hadn't been living in it for the last seven weeks so it was okay that Raiden was seeing inside.

Turning back to the window, she unlocked it and opened it just a couple of inches.

"Hold on while I get Cami on the line."

She watched as he pressed in some numbers and put the phone to his ear. She couldn't hear what he was saying, but he smiled. Then he handed the phone through the window to her.

"Here she is," he said.

Lisa put the phone up to her ear and didn't say anything.

"Lisa? Are you there?"

It was Camilla. She remembered her voice. She sounded young. She sounded happy.

"Lisa?"

"Yeah, I'm here."

"Lisa, are you okay? You sound different. Your voice is raspy. Have you been crying?"

How could she know that?

Lisa nodded. "Yes."

"Lisa, are you in your house?" Camilla asked softly. "Can you talk to me?"

Lisa turned away from the window and sat on the side of the bed, hunching down so she could whisper into the phone. "Yes, I'm in my house. Raiden's outside; he passed his phone through the window."

"He says you don't want him to come inside," Camilla whispered back.

"I don't," Lisa's whisper was even quieter.

"He says you've been in your house since Mexico and you haven't come out."

"I haven't," Lisa said in a voice that was barely there.

"Are you scared all the time?"

"Yeah." It was barely a breath of air.

"I was too," Camilla said.

"Did you have nightmares?" Lisa asked.

"Yeah. They were bad. Sometimes I had nightmares when I was awake."

"I have those too," Lisa admitted.

"Can I come and see you?" Camilla asked quietly.

"I don't want anyone to come inside my house. I'm ashamed." Lisa's voice was just a breath again.

"We're sisters," Camilla said, her voice just a whisper. "We've traveled the same road, you and I. There's no shame between sisters."

"It's bad."

"No, Lisa, the only thing that is bad were those animals in Mexico. They caused this. I'm not bad. You're not bad. They're bad. Let me come. I can help get you on the right path."

"I don't want Raiden to know," Lisa whispered again.

"Then he won't."

A small sob escaped. "Really?"

"Really. He's a man. This is in the sisterhood."

Lisa turned on her bed so she could see Raiden staring through the window, then she turned back and hunched over to whisper into the phone. "Hurry, okay?"

"I'll be there as soon as I can."

11

RAIDEN SMILED AS HE SLOUCHED OVER THE LARGE WAL-MART shopping cart in the outskirts of Tempe Arizona. His eyes flicked down to the shopping list again. Cami sure had loaded him up. He would have never guessed she'd behave like his mother, but she was showing signs of a Sato woman. The only difference was that his mother would have had him inside cleaning. He hated the fact that he wasn't. Instead, he was here, picking up supplies.

Cami's and Lisa's reunion had been a sight to behold. He hadn't been able to get Cami to jump the fence and take her out to the patio, so it had to be on the front porch. He wasn't sure that Lisa would open the door, but she had. Just the tiniest little bit, then she'd wormed her way out onto the stoop. Even though it was evening and it had cooled down, Lisa was sweating, and Raiden knew it was nerves. Cami had been good—she didn't make any sudden moves, didn't go in for a hug, even though Raiden knew that she was dying to.

Lisa was wearing the same thing she had worn the night before for dinner—the short set and the cardigan. Her hair had looked limp, and she looked scared as hell, but then she looked up and gave Cami a half-smile.

"You're dating a Navy SEAL, huh?"

She about knocked him over.

My girl is teasing Cami. Halle-fucking-lujah!

Cami immediately went with it. "I absolutely am. His name is Nicolas Hale. He was my high school sweetheart, then he showed up as part of the rescue party in Mexico, do you believe it?"

Lisa's eyes got wide, but it seemed that she'd spent her shot. She just nodded, wasn't able to say anything in return, but Cami was patient with her.

"I'm so glad you invited me here, Lisa," Cami said softly.

Lisa nodded.

"Can I come in?"

Lisa froze. She straight up froze. Then she gave a wild shake of her head.

"Lisa," Raiden said in a calming voice. "Would it be possible for you to go get the key to the back fence padlock and bring it to the patio door? That way Cami can come to the patio. She hasn't been trained to jump fences like I have."

Raiden watched her hands clenching and unclenching by her side. That was when he also noticed that the knuckles on her right hand were bruised and raw. That explained the sounds he'd heard this morning.

Dammit!

"I'm not sure." Lisa stumbled over the words.

Huh? What was she not sure of?

Raiden shook his head and got focused. "Lisa, honey, don't you want Cami to visit out on the patio?" he asked softly.

Her head jerked up to him and she gave him a confused

look, then she seemed to gather herself and she nodded. "Uhm, yeah." She turned back to Cami. "I'm really glad you came." Then Raiden was blown away when he saw her reach out and touch Cami's right hand with her left. "Thank you."

Lisa quickly turned and slipped back into her house.

That had been three hours ago. After that Raiden had gotten to watch miracles. Lisa had brought out the key and he'd opened the back fence to let Cami into the backyard. He had watched as two women bonded like they really were long-lost sisters. It had been a beautiful sight to behold. Then they'd snuck into Lisa's house, and twenty minutes later, Cami had come out with a list of supplies and he'd been sent on his way. Who knew that Wal-Mart was open until eleven o'clock at night?

"I'M TELLING YOU, I work at a university. This has nothing on college dorm rooms, let alone fraternity houses," Camilla said with a smile.

Lisa watched as Camilla pulled out a load of laundry and tossed it in the dryer, then tossed in the sheets, added some soap, and started the machine.

"Camilla—"

"You can call me Cami, all of Nic's friends do," Camilla said for the fourth time. She casually put her arm around Lisa then led her toward the dining room table that was divested of all the clutter and positioned her down into a seat. "You better sit down before you fall down."

"Cami, you're doing too much. This is my job," Lisa said for at least the fourth time.

"When you're up for it, you can come clean my house,"

Cami said with a quick smile. "Right now, you are not at your fighting weight."

Cami sat down across from her. "What do you want to eat?"

"Huh?"

"What should we have Raiden pick up for a late-night dinner? I told him what groceries to stock up on, but girlfriend, we have way too many loads of dishes to get through before we're going to be able to cook a meal. So, what do you want him to pick up for dinner?"

Lisa gripped the edges of the chair; she was feeling a little nauseous. She'd been following Cami around her house for the last hour—not that she'd been doing anything else, like bending over and picking anything up. Nope, she'd been a lump. But just walking around had taken all of her energy.

"Lisa, are you all right?"

"No."

Cami put down the phone, then was out of her chair and crouched down beside her. "What's wrong, Lisa? How did I upset you?"

"You didn't."

"Yes, I did. What did I do?"

Lisa closed her eyes, trying to think. That made her even dizzier, so she slammed her eyes open and swallowed deep. "I think I need to lay down," she whispered.

"I just bowled right over you, didn't I?" Cami cupped her jaw with her hands and Lisa didn't even flinch. It felt nice. "Raiden had said you were sleeping a lot. I didn't even take that into consideration. I'm so sorry."

"It's okay," Lisa murmured.

"No, it's not. It's late. Do you want to go to bed? Take a shower first? Do you want dinner?"

Lisa laughed. How could she help herself? Who was this woman? *I mean, I remember that Camilla Ross was in charge of all those students back in Mexico, but this powerhouse is something else.*

"You've changed," Lisa said.

"How do you mean?"

"You're kind of taking over. You're kind of pushy."

Cami gave a slow, sweet smile. "I see a lot of me in you. People have been helping me so much back in Virginia, and I'm overjoyed at the idea of being able to spread some of that help to you. So you're getting it ten times over."

"It's a lot," Lisa admitted.

"Do I need to tamp it down a bit?" Cami asked anxiously.

"Right at this minute, yes. Tomorrow, maybe not."

"Good to know. So shower, food, or bed? 'Cause I think you need to eat a little something, then have a shower, then bed."

Lisa laughed. "So really, I don't have a choice is what you're saying."

Cami tipped her head and her cheeks heated, but then she said, "Well, no, not really."

Lisa laughed again.

"I saw some tapioca in your fridge."

"Can you get me something to drink too?" Lisa asked.

"Absolutely. Then we'll get you a shower and into bed."

When Camilla went to stand up, Lisa gripped her wrist. "You won't let Raiden come inside, will you, Cami?"

"Absolutely not."

"Are you going to tell him how bad I've been living?"

Cami's eyes softened as she looked down at Lisa. "No sweetie, that's just between us girls."

"Thank you."

RAIDEN WAS LESS than happy that he couldn't take one goddamn thing into the house when he got back to Lisa's place.

"You need to dial it back," Cami said softly between the seventh and eighth load she dragged inside.

"I have dialed it back," he retorted.

"Then dial it back further, because right now your level of agitation could be measured on a Richter scale," Cami said as she put her hand on his chest.

Raiden chuckled.

"I brought some sandwiches. I thought the three of us could eat tonight." He tilted his chin toward the bags on the patio table.

"It'll just be the two of us."

"I gathered that."

"Let me just get the last of these bags into the house."

Raiden started walking the perimeter. He wanted to make sure everything was closed and locked up tight. He figured that Cami probably had Lisa settled back in the master bedroom. He glanced down at the lock on the guest bedroom window and stopped short. Lisa was sleeping in the bed. He could see that the bed had been made; it wasn't just a jumbled heap of sheets and blankets. She actually looked like someone had tucked her in. Her long dark hair was freshly washed and was fanned out over the white pillowcases.

Cami had done good.

Please Lord, let Lisa not have any nightmares.

The phone in his back pocket vibrated and he grabbed it, hoping it was Harry. He smiled when he saw it was.

"You almost here?" he asked.

"Well, since you told me that I had to be, I figured I didn't have a choice," Harry Chapman said wryly.

Raiden laughed into his phone.

"Took you long enough."

"Man, you called me this morning. I actually have duties, I can't just take off whenever the hell I want. Plus, my wife likes it when I discuss things with her, not just take off. I find it helps keep our marriage a good one."

Raiden laughed again.

"So you want me to play babysitter, do I have that right?"

"Basically. Just should be for a day or two. But if you could not use that term, I'd be much obliged."

"I have been hearing about your team all pairing up. So you now have a woman that needs to be watched after, is that the deal?"

"This is Nic Hale's woman. Him and the rest of Night Storm are overseas, I took leave to lend a hand on a situation here in Tempe. Camilla Ross, Nic's woman, is here to help. I need you to look after her while I stay here with Lisa."

"So is Lisa yours?" Harry asked.

"It's complicated," Raiden answered.

Harry sighed. "It always is."

"I just appreciate you being able to pull away from base. You're the only one I knew who was close."

"Hell, Raiden, there are plenty of guys in any arm of the services who would be more than happy to have your back, all you ever have to do is make a call. Fort Huachuca is just one of many places you could tap."

It felt good to hear.

"I should be pulling off the highway in about ten minutes; what do I need to know?"

"I'm staying here with Lisa. I've got you and Camilla

booked at the Marriott. I want her covered coming and going."

"Is there a reason why you're so concerned about security? Not that I think it's wrong, considering the fact I'm in Military Intelligence I always think security is a good thing, but just saying, escorting a lady to and from a hotel could seem, to some people, a little over the top."

"That's another reason I called you. Lisa called in to the sheriff a little less than two weeks ago. She thought she heard something. When they looked around they didn't see any footprints, but they did say there had been a disturbance. I'd like you to find out what you can about their report."

"So there *is* something," Harry said.

"I've just got a feeling on this. I can't explain it. Lisa's been in a bad way since we rescued her in Mexico. Total PTSD. I'm sure they brushed it under the rug. But too much has happened to her, she can't take another hit, so she won't. You hear me?"

"I hear you. And Nic's wife?"

"She's not his wife yet. Her name is Camilla Ross. She was rescued down in Mexico too. But they have a long past. They knew each other six years ago. My guess is he'll have his ring on her finger before a year is out."

Harry chuckled. "Good man. So what's your concern with her?"

"She's here to support Lisa. She dropped everything to be here. She's just pulling out after all she went through down there, so I want to make sure that somebody's got her back, while I'm here at Lisa's house."

"Is there a reason you're not all just staying at Lisa's?"

"Yeah."

"You going to tell me?" Harry asked.

"No."

"Well okay then."

Raiden smiled. Harry was wrong; there might be a lot of men he could've tapped to help him out, but not many like Harry who would know which questions to ask and which ones not to ask.

12

It was past midnight. Harry had taken Cami to the Marriott. She'd been nice about it, but she'd still given Raiden a look that said they'd be having words later. He really didn't care, as long as she was safe. That's all he wanted, everyone to be safe.

Once again he left the lounge chair close to the guest bedroom window so he could hear Lisa if she needed him during the night. He hadn't gotten a whole hell of a lot of sleep last night, so he skipped reading a book, and instead just let himself drift.

"Raiden?"

He didn't open his eyes, though his body was on instant alert. Then he rolled over as he realized Lisa's voice had come from the living room and she was walking toward the patio door. He sat up.

"Yeah, honey?"

He heard the door open a little bit.

"Uhm."

He waited, not wanting to do anything that might throw

her off course. This was her play. But then when she didn't say anything else, he finally said her name again.

"Lisa?"

"You sleeping?" she asked.

"Nope. Wanna come on out?"

"Yeah." She sounded relieved at his answer.

He pushed up out of the sleeping bag and wished he had a shirt on. Being a guide, she had to have seen a lot of men without their shirts, but right now, he didn't think this was a great idea. He leaned over to his backpack and snagged it, grabbing a t-shirt and shoving his arms into it before she came out onto the patio.

"Where's Camilla?"

"She had a reservation at a hotel. She'll be back tomorrow morning," he assured her.

Lisa gave a half smile as she sat down on the edge of the chair. What he wouldn't give to see a full smile from this woman.

"Thank you for having Camilla come here," she said quietly. He watched as she pushed her pretty, dark-brown hair off her face and looked out over her backyard, out into the night sky.

"You're welcome," he responded just as quietly.

He turned his head away from her even though he didn't want to so that he could look at the night sky as well.

"I've never met somebody as patient as you are."

Raiden laughed but continued to look at the stars.

"Why are you laughing?"

"Because I'm not that patient. You should ask my cousin Leif. Trust me, I can be pretty damned impatient."

He looked at her out of the corner of his eye, hoping that he hadn't scared her. By the looks of things, he hadn't.

"But you're patient with me."

"Yep."

"Why?"

"Honey, that's what you need."

"You also make me feel safe. Do you always make everybody feel safe?"

"Nope." Again he glanced over at her and saw her chewing on his answer.

"Raiden?"

"Right here," he smiled.

"You've made me think that I'm important to you."

This time he turned back to her so he could look at her straight on. "Then I'm doing my job right."

His jaw clenched and his hands fisted when he saw her eyes welling up with tears.

"I'm not important." Her voice was low.

"Depends who's doing the looking, Lisa. I've thought you were important and special from the moment I clapped eyes on you."

She continued to stare at him. No single tear fell, but he could see how it was killing her to hold them in.

"How'd you end up in foster care?"

He could have asked Kane to give him the lowdown. Maybe he should have. But he'd really wanted to hear it from her. He wanted to have her share with him, but hearing this kind of deep-down hurt, maybe he should have probed.

"I didn't go in until I was sixteen," she whispered.

"Isn't that kind of late?" *Shit, that was a stupid question.* "I mean, what happened?"

Her lip twitched up. "Probably the best thing that ever happened to me was going into foster care at sixteen."

Raiden was careful this time before saying anything. "Why is that, honey?"

"I was raised by my mom's mom. It wasn't good with her. It was better being away."

"Lisa, that's saying an awful lot in just three sentences."

She bent forward in the chair, her hair hiding her face. "She didn't like me much."

"Did she hurt you?"

She bent forward even more.

"Sometimes. Not as much as I grew up."

Fuck!

"So nobody intervened until you were sixteen?"

Her harsh laugh hit him in the gut.

"Nobody intervened, period. She kicked me out."

She was killing him, but he had to know. There were too many puzzle pieces that were missing and he had to find them.

"Why, baby? Why would she kick you out? That makes no sense."

"Sure it does. When the police drove me home that night and told her what happened, she called me trash. Called me a slut. Said I was asking for it. Threw my stuff out on the lawn. Said I was just like my mom."

He looked at her sitting there hunched over, her long hair swinging down almost to the ground, her arms clasped around her middle, and somehow he was kneeling in front of her. He didn't touch her. He was too afraid.

"Lisa, can you lift your head and look at me?"

She shook her head.

"Please, darlin' I'm begging you." He heard the hoarseness in his voice.

"I don't want you to see me."

"I've got to see your eyes. Please let me see your beautiful brown eyes."

Slowly, as if her head weighed a thousand pounds, she raised her neck. Then her eyes met his.

"You're special."

She stared at him. Raiden didn't even know if she was seeing him.

"Lisa Garcia, you're special. You're special and important to me."

"There's something wrong with me, Raiden." Her voice sounded dead.

"No, Lisa, there is nothing, absolutely nothing, wrong with you. You're special. Light shines from you. I saw it in Mexico. You're fierce and brave and beautiful and special."

Her head started to lower and his hand shot up, two fingers touching her chin. She stayed with him, not moving. "God put you on this earth for a reason. You're special."

She reached up and encircled his wrist. Raiden thought she was going to pull him away, that he'd screwed up. Instead, she clung.

"I don't want to go back inside."

"Then don't. Sleep out here tonight. Under the stars."

Her eyes darted to the lounge chair.

"Where will *you* sleep?"

"I won't. I have a book to finish. Let's get you settled. Okay?"

She looked up at him, giving him a searching gaze. She must have seen what she needed to see because she nodded and released her hold.

He stood up and held out his hand to her. He was damn near holding his breath, and when she put her small hand in his, his heart clenched. Raiden helped her up. He was careful not to touch her any other way as he escorted her the few feet to the sleeping bag on the lounge chair.

"Do you want me to go inside and get you a pillow?" he asked.

She shook her head. "Not yet. We're still not done in there. Anyway, the chair is padded."

Raiden watched as she snuggled into the sleeping bag. Her fingers folded over the top and she looked up at him, her face pale in the starlight.

"Raiden?"

"Right here."

"It's nice you think I'm special. I'm going to hate it when you find out I'm not."

His eyes squeezed shut for just an instant. Then he crouched down.

"I'm going to love it when you find out for yourself, that you *are* special. Sweet dreams, Lisa."

LISA WOKE UP CONFUSED. The sun was shining on her, and she felt rested.

"Lisa honey? You awake now?"

She turned her head and saw Raiden, and last night came flooding back to her. She wanted to pull the sleeping bag over her head. How could she have opened up as much as she had?

"Harry is dropping off Cami in a few minutes. She'll be bringing breakfast."

She pushed back the sleeping bag and lifted her head.

"Harry?" she asked.

"He's a buddy of mine from Fort Huachuca over in Cochise. He's staying at the Marriott with Cami."

Lisa let that information settle. It didn't make any sense. Why would Raiden's friend be staying at the same hotel as

Camilla? She needed coffee to help her think. Lisa's shoulders jerked and her eyes got wide.

"What is it, honey?"

She saw that Raiden was carefully watching her.

"I just had a craving for coffee," she whispered. "I haven't wanted coffee since Mexico."

She watched as he slowly smiled. "Well that's a very good thing, now isn't it?"

"I really think it is. Who is Harry?"

"I told you, he's a friend of mine."

She unzipped the sleeping bag and slid her legs over the side of the lounge chair. "Yeah, I got that part, but where did he come from, and why is he at the Marriott with Camilla?"

Raiden rubbed his jaw and watched her.

"Are you going to answer me?"

"You wake up feisty, don't you?"

She used to. She used to be a morning person. She remembered that. She also remembered that she wouldn't let someone get away with not answering a simple question.

"Raiden, tell me why your friend is staying at the Marriott with Cami."

"I didn't like the sound of your prowler. Plus, Nic would hand me my ass if I was having Cami driving around a strange town at night to go to her hotel when she's still recovering from Mexico. Therefore I called in Harry."

"All the way from Cochise? That's two hours from here. You should have driven her to the hotel."

His brown eyes flared. "I wasn't going to leave you, Lisa."

"That's stupid. It's how long to get to the hotel? Thirty minutes? You'd only be gone for an hour."

He crossed his arms over his chest. His massive chest. The chest that she'd seen naked last night for just a moment. "I wasn't going to leave you." This time his words came out as a rumble.

Lisa jumped at the sound of a car horn honking. Raiden grinned. "Guess we're not arguing anymore, food is here."

"We weren't arguing," Lisa argued.

He grinned. "Whatever you need to believe, honey."

He turned to the gate and Lisa panicked. "You're not going to let Harry in, are you?"

"No, Lisa, I'm not. He's just dropping Cami off. He's going back to the hotel to get some work done. He'll come back tonight to pick her up."

Lisa gave him an incredulous look. "Wait a minute, are you seriously telling me that he is nothing but a glorified Uber driver? Are you out of your mind?"

Raiden let out a loud laugh. "There's my girl. I knew she was hiding in there."

Lisa's eyes narrowed. "What are you talking about?"

"Always knew you were full of piss and vinegar. I like it. Now let me let Cami in." He turned away from her and she sat there stunned. He was right. She had actually gotten upset with him. A big man. She was outside of her house giving 'what-for' to a big man. She wasn't hyperventilating and getting ready to scurry back inside; instead, she was waiting for him to come back so she could either find out what was for breakfast or continue their argument.

Her fingers touched her lips as she felt the beginnings of a small smile. Maybe things would get better.

IT WAS nice listening to Camilla and Raiden talk about all of Raiden's team members. Plus there was the added advantage that she didn't really need to enter the conversation. After the morning spent cleaning, an early lunch on the patio was relaxing. Raiden had gone to his motel and showered after physical training and he was looking... Well, Lisa didn't quite know how to describe how he looked.

She kept taking surreptitious glances at him underneath her lashes. He was wearing some kind of silver athletic shirt that looked like it had been painted onto his body, that along with cargo shorts and running shoes. This wasn't like her; she never looked at men. She didn't. Never. Ever. But she was now. Then there was his voice. It was smooth and warm. But last night and this morning she'd heard it rumble. She'd liked it both ways. Even when it rumbled, his voice had never scared her.

"—is taking another shift today, I'll call her tonight."

Lisa looked over at Camilla, trying to catch onto what she was saying.

"What about your classes, do you need to get back to them?" Raiden asked.

Camilla laughed. "Nah, I'm not due to teach until next term. Right now I'm just counseling. As long as I have a phone and e-mail, I'm good to stay."

"You don't have to stay with me," Lisa chimed in. "You can go home tonight." She set down her half-eaten tuna sandwich on the paper bag and gave Cami a half-hearted smile.

"I want to stay. Anyway, Nic wants me to be around people while he's out on his first mission. He'd probably like this better anyway, since Carys is at the hospital so much. They are so short-staffed, they're giving her double shifts."

"Does Cullen know about this?" Raiden asked.

"How could he, he's on a mission?"

"Does this happen when he's home?" Raiden persisted.

"No," Cami admitted.

"Didn't think so. He wouldn't want anyone taking advantage of her. Yeah, if they were really in a pinch once, he'd understand, but on a continual basis, no way. I'll give Cullen a call and let him know what's up," Raiden said.

Cami gave him a startled look. "You can't do that."

"Oh yeah, I can. The hospital is taking advantage of Carys, and he needs to know about it."

"But he's on a mission," Cami protested.

"Let me worry about that." He looked at Cami's empty wrapper. "Are you done with lunch?"

Cami nodded.

"What about you, honey?" he asked Lisa in a softer voice.

"This is all I can eat. I'll put the rest in the refrigerator."

"I'll tell you what. You ladies go in and clean, and I'll make some calls. Then later tonight before Cami goes back to her hotel, I'll have Harry come on by early so I can take a run."

"Raiden, isn't that a little overboard? You can go for a run now. Lisa and I will be just fine. After all, you went to your motel earlier and were gone for forty-five minutes," Cami said.

"Yeah, but it'll be dusk when I'm running, and I'll be gone for two hours. We'll wait for Harry."

Cami looked at Lisa and rolled her eyes. Lisa giggled for the first time in eight weeks. They got up and went into the house to hopefully do the last bit of cleaning.

Please God say it was the last bit.

13

"WHO DO YOU THINK HE'S OUT THERE TALKING TO?" LISA asked. "He sounds kind of angry."

Camilla's lips twitched. "According to the rumor mill he's trying to kick his younger cousin's ass and bring him back into the family fold. The kid needs it."

Lisa looked back out into the backyard as she folded another piece of laundry. Then she saw Raiden's lip twitch and his eyes turn heavenward. Okay, maybe he wasn't really as angry as he was sounding.

"Raiden likes his family," Lisa said.

"He told you that?" Cami asked.

"Yes."

"What else did he tell you about himself?" Cami probed.

Lisa looked across the guestroom bed where Cami was folding clothes too. "Why are you asking?"

"Just wondering what you and Raiden have been talking about for the three days before I got here."

"Uhm, not a lot really. He spent a lot of time just trying to get me to come out of the house. I guess he was mostly reassuring."

Cami looked down at the bedspread. "I could see that."

"It's all folded. What day is today?"

"Day of the week, or date?"

"Day of the week," Lisa clarified.

"Thursday."

"Tomorrow is garbage pick-up." Lisa bit her lip.

Cami's head immediately shot up and Lisa saw she understood. "Honey, Raiden can take the cans out to the curb. Or I can."

Lisa straightened her shoulders. "No. I'm going to do it."

"We'll both do it," Camilla said firmly.

Lisa released a sigh of relief. "Okay."

They went to the bags of trash piled up next to the carport door and pushed them aside. Lisa opened the door and saw flies buzzing around her recycle and trash bin. They stank.

"Camilla, let me do this. They stink."

"We were in Mexico together, I can handle this just fine," Cami grinned.

Lisa stepped back inside and got two more bags of trash and swung them up into the trash bin then shoved them down into the big bin, barely getting the lid to close. "I'll take this one, you take the recycling," she told Cami.

"Okay."

As she started down her long drive to the curb, she looked over her neighborhood for the first time in almost two months. Nothing really had changed. Not a lot of cars were in the drives, mostly in garages or carports. She saw one van for window cleaning, two beat-up little trucks that were local gardeners, then there was a nicer panel van that said it was a lawn care service.

She was the only person in the neighborhood who actually took care of her own yard; it was just the way it was.

"Is that lady waving at you?" Cami asked as they positioned the bins at the curb.

Lisa turned to see Mrs. Curruthers waving to her on her walkway. Lisa waved back and smiled. Now she had to get the hell back to her house, it was too much. Cami must have seen it. "You're doing good, Lisa. We'll just go back now."

"Excuse me, is this your house?" Lisa had been so busy concentrating on Mrs. Curruthers she hadn't noticed the white lawn care truck pulling up. A nice Hispanic man was smiling at her and Cami out of the passenger side window, pointing up at her house.

"Yes, it's my house. I don't need lawn care." Lisa knew her voice was trembling. She grabbed Cami's hand. She needed to get back into the house.

Now!

She couldn't handle talking to another person. She needed to get back inside.

The side of the panel van opened and two men jumped out.

"Which one?" One of the two men asked his partner.

What are they talking about? Then she realized they were looking between her and Cami. She backed away, and so did Cami.

"Take 'em both." The guy on the right said.

"No, take me," Lisa cried.

"No, me," Cami said as she pushed Lisa aside.

This couldn't be actually happening. Please God say it's not happening.

Lisa looked at the man who had his hand around Cami's bicep. She lowered her head and charged into his chest as she screamed, "Raiden!"

Hands grabbed at her, ripping at her hair.

"Raiden!" Now it just wasn't her screaming, it was Cami too.

The man ripped Lisa off her feet and threw her into the back of the van. The door slid shut. She screamed Raiden's name again. She looked around wildly. Even in the darkness, she didn't see Cami, but she could be wrong.

"Cami, are you here?" she yelled.

"Shut her up!"

A fist hit the side of her head, then nothing.

RAIDEN PULLED Cami up off the ground onto his thighs. Her head was bleeding.

"Call nine-one-one," he shouted at the old lady who was rushing to him.

"Who were those men?" the lady shouted.

"Call nine-one-one," he shouted again.

She looked into his eyes, nodded, then ran back to her house.

Cami's eyelids fluttered up. "White van, Rainbow Landscape," she whispered.

He looked down the street and saw nothing. His eyes went back to her as his fingers traced the back of her head. He found where her head had hit the pavement. He probed carefully. No fracture.

"I'm good," she said.

"No, you're not."

"I am. Go after Lisa."

"Police and ambulance are on their way," the lady shouted out from her doorstep. Raiden gave her a chin tilt, then focused back on Cami.

"Help will be here soon."

"Go after Lisa."

"I will."

Her hand reached up and grabbed his wrist. "Go help Lisa, they've got her!" Tears spilled from her eyes, tracking down her cheeks.

"I will, Cami, I promise."

She slumped back and rested her head on his thigh. Raiden wiped his bloody hands off on his cargo shorts, then pulled his phone out of one of his pockets. He pulled up his recent contacts and got Harry on the line.

"Harry, Lisa has been kidnapped. I need you to stay on the line while I see if I can get our comm guy on. He's overseas, but they shouldn't be seeing action for another thirty-six hours."

"Gotcha," Harry answered.

Raiden stroked Cami's hair as he looked down at her ashen face. *The ambulance better get here pretty fucking quick.*

He hit the keys to do a three-way call, then tried to patch in Kane.

"Fuck," he murmured as it went to voicemail.

"Kane, call me. It's urgent."

He clicked back to Harry. "Kane's unavailable. I'm going to pull in either Clint or Dex from California."

"I can help," Harry said.

"I know you're Military Intelligence. I know you can help, and I want you to. That's why we're going to have a joint call. But you gather intel, we do ops." He clicked away and went through his contacts. It was Clint, since his last name was Archer and he came up first.

Where are the sirens?

"Raiden?" Clint answered.

"Yeah, in Arizona. Got a situation. A kidnapping. You available to help?"

"Yep."

"Patching you into a friend of mine who's with me, Army Military Intelligence, Harry Chapman."

"Link us up," Clint said immediately.

Raiden pressed his fingers against Cami's throat. Her pulse was good. She moaned.

"Stick with me, Cami. Help's on the way."

He connected the calls.

"You both on?" He heard them both say yeah. "Harry Chapman, Military Intelligence, out of Arizona. Clint Archer, Navy SEAL communications expert out of Coronado. The situation is this. Lisa Garcia, twenty-seven, recently rescued from kidnappers in Mexico, by my team. She took out one of the leaders. According to the local federales, none of the kidnappers made it out alive, we took them at their word, never confirmed. I'm thinking this is payback for her role in killing the leader."

"Why not just a hit?" Chapman asked.

"When was this mission exactly?" Clint asked.

"The mission was eight weeks ago. You should be able to go to Captain Hale and get the info," he told Clint. "Harry, the fact that it was a kidnapping and not a hit is the reason I think these two things are related. This is a grudge. Someone wants to take revenge, and my guess is they want to see her suffer."

"That's good then," Clint said. "Means we have some time."

Raiden closed his eyes at the thought of Lisa suffering. Then he heard sirens.

"I have a witness with me. Her name is Camilla Ross. She was hurt during the kidnapping. She said that they were driving a white van, saying Rainbow Landscape. The police are arriving; they'll be combing the neighborhood to see what they know. If either of you could tap into that info, that would be great."

"What are you going to be doing?" Clint asked.

"I'm going to the hospital with Cami. After that, I'm going to find these motherfuckers."

"WHERE IS OUR MONEY?" a man asked in Spanish.

"Just calm down, you'll get your money," another man replied in Spanish. He sounded bored.

"I'm not going to calm down. Do you know what kind of time I could do for kidnapping? This is bullshit, I want my fucking money, and I want it now!"

She drew in a shaky breath and realized all of her clothes were on, and no one was touching her. A tear of relief seeped through her blindfold. Somebody wanted money for her. Nobody was touching her. She could deal with this.

I can.

Lisa's whole body shook at the sound of a gun going off. Was that the sound of a body hitting the floor? It sounded like it had happened right beside her, but she couldn't see anything. She couldn't even scream because she had a gag in her mouth.

"Now, does anybody else want to voice a complaint?" the bored man asked.

There was silence.

"Answer me!"

Lisa heard three men say no.

Lisa shuddered, praying that she wasn't going to be shot next.

"Now tell me again how you fucked up," the bored man said. "Tell me again how you left a witness."

"We didn't. She's dead."

"Not according to the police band radio." Now he didn't sound so bored.

He was talking about Camilla. Thank God, she was alive. She hadn't been kidnapped. She was alive and hadn't been kidnapped. Okay, things were going to be okay. Lisa could deal with this now. She just needed to stay alive and Raiden would come and get her.

"Well if she's not dead, we'll take care of it."

"Damn right you will," bored guy with a gun said. "You won't be getting your money for a sloppy job."

"Wait a minute, you were supposed to take her off our hands." Someone pushed Lisa's back with the toe of their boot.

"And I will, when the time is right. It isn't right. You've been paid well up-front for your job so far. Plus it now only has to be divided up three ways. You keep her in pristine condition for the next two days, tie up the loose ends you created, and I'll take her off your hands then."

"We're not a babysitting service. You didn't tell us about holding her for two days."

"Adapt."

"If we're caught with her, we'll go down for life," one of the men whined.

"Then my advice is to not get caught."

Lisa heard a door closing.

"Fuck," one of the men said.

"Who's going to clean up Alberto?"

"Not me. I had to get lunch. Plus I gassed up the van. One of you guys has to clean up the dead body."

Was he for real?

"What about her?" another guy asked.

"Shit, I'm not set up to be a babysitter, but I can get my old lady to come. She won't say shit because she's counting on the money."

"You trust her?" It was the guy who'd gotten lunch.

"Been married to her for years. Won't be the first time she's had to help me out of a jam. So since I'm getting Nellie to do the babysitting and you got lunch, that means Rick has to clean up the dead body."

"Shit," Rick said. "Next time I'll remember to buy lunch."

14

"SHE HAS A CONCUSSION, WE'RE KEEPING HER HERE overnight," the doctor said to Raiden and Harry.

Carys would be flying into Phoenix that evening. Raiden wasn't happy about it, not happy one bit, but there hadn't been a damn thing he could do to stop her. Clint was driving in with his wife Lydia, so they should be here about the same damn time. Why in the hell Clint was bringing his wife made no sense to Raiden, but whatever, as long as Clint was getting here. But that still left him here at the hospital with his thumb up his ass.

When his phone vibrated and he saw it was Kane he sent a prayer of thanks up to Heaven and walked away from the doctor and Harry.

"What the fuck?" Kane said.

"I told you in the voicemail."

"And I repeat, what the fucking fuck?"

"Cami has a concussion; she's spending the night here in the hospital for observation. The cops have a partial on the van's plate from somebody's doorbell camera. They're still running that down. What we have from Cami is at least three Hispanic men, she couldn't ID the driver."

"And?" Kane growled.

"It's got to be tied to our Mexico op. I figure that Maria bitch got away. She's holding a grudge against Lisa for killing the boss."

"Goddamn federales. Never should have trusted their intel."

"Got that right," Raiden agreed.

"Okay, what do you need from me?" Kane asked.

"Just so we're not walking over everybody, I've already pulled in Harry Chapman from Military Intelligence out of Fort Huachuca and Clint Archer."

"Okay, at least Clint's a SEAL and he's from Midnight Delta, but I don't know Harry," Kane said.

"He's an old friend who is stationed here in Arizona. I needed some more boots on the ground to cover Cami while I stayed with Lisa at her house, so I pulled him in."

"Is he good?" Kane asked.

"Absolutely. Problem is, he's not used to field ops, just intelligence gathering. That's why I pulled in Clint Archer. But fuck-all if I know why he's driving in with his wife."

Kane chuckled. "Lydia is the shit. Seriously, it's like you'll have Clint squared. Trust me, you'll be happy to have her. So they're driving over? What's their E.T.A.?"

Raiden looked down at his watch. Goddammit, four hours had gone by since Lisa had been snatched!

"They should be here in two more hours."

"I'll get on the phone with them and give them everything I have on the Mexico op, including where I think the fuck-up happened with the federales. I agree with you— this is probably the Maria woman, but because we thought she was dead, we didn't do an in-depth ID on her."

Raiden clamped down his rage. Just one simple mistake like that, and they were here. Kane must have known what he was thinking.

"It's okay, man, we'll get it taken care of. Does Cami have her phone with her?"

"No, but I'll text you with the hospital info and room number."

"No, text it straight to Nic," Kane instructed.

"Gotcha."

———

"You awake?" The words were in accented English.

Lisa didn't make a move. Didn't make a sound. She tried not to even breathe.

"You're awake." She was hauled up by her armpits and shoved up against a wall into a seated position. "I'm not going to take off your blindfold, but if you promise not to scream, I'll take off your gag. Okay?" All of these questions were asked in English. It was the man who had the old lady named Nellie.

Lisa nodded. A coil of fear rose in her belly but she clamped it down. Hard. She could get through this. Nobody was touching her. She just had to keep telling herself that nobody was touching her, and everything would be all right.

When the man took off her gag, she wiggled her jaw to loosen it. "Thirsty."

"If you do what I tell you to do, I'll give you some water. Nod if you understand me."

Lisa nodded.

"Nothing's going to happen to you. You're going to be just fine. All you have to do is be cool for a couple of days, then we're going to send you back to your people. Do you understand?"

Lisa didn't move, she waited.

"Nod, goddammit."

Lisa jumped. Then she nodded. "Can I have some water?"

He thrust a bottle of water into her chest. She tried to grab at it, but her hands were tied together, so when she went to grab for the bottle it dropped to the ground. Tears of frustration welled behind her blindfold. She breathed through her nose, thinking of Alaska and everything she was capable of. Dammit, she used to climb mountains. She had rescued people. If all she had to deal with was a blindfold in a hot room, she could deal with this.

Breathe.

"For fuck's sake, what's your problem?"

Lisa didn't say anything. She didn't want to make the man mad, but she wanted the water.

"Can you help me with the water?" she asked carefully.

Strong hands grabbed her arms and she felt a tug, then her hands were free. "There, maybe you can hold a bottle of water now." He thrust the bottle into her hands. She touched it and identified the cap, then twisted it off. She took a long pull, then another.

"That's enough. We're going to take you someplace else with a bathroom. Don't have one here, so don't be drinking too much."

She had two days before she was going to be released to a murderer. The coil of fear started slithering through her belly.

Then she felt it, and she wanted to cry. With the blindfold on, Lisa felt herself getting dizzy and she gritted her teeth so it wouldn't happen. She'd spent damn near two months being tired, dizzy, and helpless as she spiraled into despair. With Raiden, Cami, a few good meals, and some sleep she was finally coming out of it, and she was not going to sink back into it now!

Nobody had tried to rape her. Nobody had attempted to kill her...yet. Raiden was out there and he was a SEAL, he'd saved her before. She had two days before the murderer was coming back for her so there was still hope. She'd come back from the edge before, she could do it again.

Someone grabbed her feet and there was another tug, then she realized that her legs were no longer tied together. "Get up."

She was yanked up by her armpits again into a standing position. The world spun and she gagged. The water bottle fell to the floor.

"Don't vomit on me!"

"Don't move me around so fast when I'm blindfolded," she shot back.

He yanked her across the floor then pushed her down. She was now on some kind of soft chair or sofa. "Stay there."

"How long have I been here?" she asked.

She felt him sit beside her on the couch. He didn't answer her. Then she heard the distinctive sounds of a kid's video game. If she had to guess it was Grand Theft Auto. *How appropriate.*

As soon as she felt herself sinking into the cushions, she stopped herself. She pushed upright. She was not going to allow herself to do one thing that seemed like giving up. She was going to stay alert. Behind the blindfold, she conjured up Raiden's face like she had seen him the other night under the stars.

"Lisa, you are special."

She held onto those words.

"TALK TO ME," Raiden demanded.

"The van was stolen. It was found abandoned outside of Tucson." Lydia Archer answered as she looked up from her laptop.

Just looking at the beautiful Hispanic woman seated in Lisa's home made Raiden's heart hurt.

"Prints?" Harry asked.

"The cops haven't processed it yet," Clint answered. "We'll know as soon as they know."

"I don't want to know how you're doing this," Harry said with his hands up.

"We won't tell you," Lydia said with her head down.

Clint looked up at Harry from his laptop on the other side of the dining room table. "Harry, Lyd and I are about an hour away from getting into the Mexican federales system, but that is only going to tell us what they reported, not what really happened. Do you have any sources down there?"

Harry stood up and took out his phone. "Let me make a couple of phone calls. I might."

Clint nodded.

Raiden waited until Harry had walked away, then he spoke low to Clint and Lydia. After talking to Kane, he realized that Lydia had been working as a quasi-member of Midnight Delta for years. He didn't quite understand it, but he wasn't going to argue anything that worked at this point in the game.

"I talked to Max," Raiden said. "He's having Captain Hale push to get info. The man is fucking pissed about what happened to Cami. Harry might have connections, but Nic's father is going to cut through everything and find out what the fuck went on down there. I'm positive this comes down to that bitch Maria. I need to find out more about her when I go back to see Cami in the hospital tonight. But the Captain is going to find out Maria's connections and where the hell she is."

Lydia looked up from her laptop. "You're going to go easy on her, right?"

Raiden gave her an incredulous look. "Of course I am."

Clint gave Raiden a stand-down look, and Raiden took a deep breath. "Sorry, Lydia. You don't know me, sorry if I'm coming off too strong. But of course, I'm going to go in gentle with Cami."

She smiled and nodded.

"Okay, that's one half of the puzzle," Clint nodded. "But according to Cami's statement, there wasn't a woman in that van, so Maria didn't do the kidnapping. They still have to get Lisa in front of Maria. This is good news, Raiden."

"Right," Raiden gritted out.

"It is," Lydia said as she put her hand on top of his. "Your girl is strong; she's going to do everything to stay alive, and we got in on this quick. We'll find her."

Raiden closed his eyes. He wished that were true. But Lisa was barely back on her feet and the idea of her being captured again? It would devastate her. Even if she came out of this alive, how could she ever recover?

A DOOR OPENED and the video game shut off. "Baby, thank God you're here," the man said in Spanish.

"What in the hell have you gotten me into this time?" a woman asked.

"Nellie, I need your help. We've got a situation."

"A woman is tied up, gagged, and blindfolded on a couch

here. I can see we have a damned situation." She was growling.

"Please don't be mad, darlin'. I'll make it up to you. You know this deal is worth a lot of cash."

"Jesus Christ, Mel. You've got a woman blindfolded on the couch. She's not here of her own free will. What in the hell are you thinking? Let her go, I don't care how much money this deal is worth, I don't want any part of it."

Lisa heard the door opening. The woman was planning on leaving. Lisa didn't want to be left alone. She pulled at the bindings on her wrists. He'd put on another set of zip-ties after she'd had her water. Same with her ankles.

"Alberto said he knows where we live," the man whispered.

"Who knows where we live?"

"The guy who shot and killed Alberto today. He killed him in cold blood. He knows where we live, Nellie. Where our kids live. We gotta do what he says."

The door slammed shut.

"What have you done, baby?" Her words were a horrified whisper.

Lisa turned her body on the couch like she wanted to look at the fool who would put his wife and kids in danger like this. What kind of idiot does this?

"I got in too deep, Alberto tapped me because I knew the neighborhood that she lived in. You know, Los Cabos Heights. I do landscaping out there. I didn't know what was coming down. It was going to pay our expenses for a year, Nellie."

"Didn't you think that something with that kind of payoff would land you in prison? Jesus, you never think, Mel. You never think."

"You gotta help me. I promised to take care of her. I

figured between you and me we could keep her alive, then we wouldn't get in trouble. Right?"

"Just call the cops."

"No, I gotta deliver her to the guy day after tomorrow," he whispered. "He said she had to be in pristine condition."

"Mel!" she screamed. "Think! You're handing her off to be killed."

"We don't know that," he whispered.

"What in the hell else could it be? You already said he's a stone-cold killer. He killed Alberto, he wants you to hand her over in two days. Of course, she's going to die."

"Why would he want her in pristine condition?" Mel argued.

Lisa heard Nellie walk over to the couch. She was close. "Mel, think, baby. It's not good. We've got to call the cops."

"I'm already an accessory to kidnapping. He'll come and kill you and our kids."

"Are you sure he knows where we live?"

"Alberto said he made it his business to know everything about the four of us. This guy is part of a cartel out of Mexico, that's how they operate."

"The cops will protect us."

"The cops won't do shit. It's the Mexican cartel baby!"

There was the longest silence imaginable.

"What do you need me to do Mel?" she asked.

It was after visiting hours, but Carys got him in. Cami wasn't sleeping anyway. She was too agitated. Raiden stopped short when he saw A.J. McNamara, Kane's wife, on the other side of Cami's bed.

"What are you doing here?" he asked.

"I'm here to help."

He wasn't sure how she could, but he'd take any help he could get.

"What have you found out?" Cami asked as she sat up in the hospital bed.

"We've got some leads. I need to know more about Maria. Anything you can tell me about her will help."

"Maria?" Cami looked confused. "You think this is about Mexico?"

Raiden nodded.

"Nic told me that everyone was killed, including her."

"We're not so sure."

"Raiden, she's evil. I mean she is truly evil. I don't mean the kind of person who was sick in the head. She was someone who liked doing evil things. She wanted people to be hurt. She got off on causing pain."

Raiden kept his expression blank. "What else can you tell me?"

"She was in love with the leader. She would have done anything for him."

"Is that the man that Lisa killed?"

Cami's already-pale face went white. She nodded, then winced with pain. "Yes," she gasped. "Maria saw Lisa shoot him. She got away. But Nic told me that everyone was killed. That meant Maria was killed, Raiden. Maria was killed." The last three words were filled with desperation.

"Maybe she was, sweetie," Raiden tried to console her.

Cami took a deep breath, then looked Raiden straight in the eye. "But you don't think so, do you?"

Raiden shook his head.

"Maria wasn't in the van," Cami said slowly. "Do you think they're taking Lisa to her?"

"I can't be sure."

"But that's what you think, isn't it?"

"Yes."

"You've got to find her before they hand her over to Maria. Raiden, you have to. It will be bad. Really bad. You can't let Maria get Lisa."

Bile hit the back of Raiden's throat. "I won't," he promised, praying he could keep that promise.

Chapter Fifteen

Raiden picked up the call from Clint as he was driving back from the hospital. A.J. was in the seat next to him.

"What do you have for me?" he asked.

"Lots of prints in the van. Two were in the system."

"And?" Raiden asked.

"One's in Phoenix. One's here in Tempe. The cops are waiting on warrants."

"Fuck that noise. I'm closer to Phoenix, text me the address. You take Tempe. Harry's out, he can't be down with this, Clint."

"I'm leaving him here with Lydia. Even though he's looking at me, he's really on the patio listening to headphones."

"Good."

Raiden handed A.J. his phone. "Plug the address into the navigation system as soon as Clint texts it to me," he requested.

She nodded.

"You're going to Denny's."

She sighed. "I prefer I-HOP."

"Let me put it this way; you're going to whatever damn restaurant is open on the next exit," he growled.

"You do know I can fire a gun, right?"

Raiden rolled his eyes as he put on his blinker.

"I never get to have any fun anymore," she said.

When they got off the freeway, the first restaurant was an I-HOP. "Oh goodie," A.J. said. "Blueberry pancakes." She had her seatbelt undone and the car door open before Raiden had the car stopped.

"Dammit, A.J.," he bit out. "Be careful."

"Find those motherfuckers," she glared at him.

"Got it."

He roared out of the parking lot and headed toward Phoenix.

Raiden kept telling himself that just because some guy's fingerprints were in the van, it didn't mean he had anything to do with the kidnapping. He told himself that all the way to the rundown house on the outskirts of Phoenix. Hell, it looked like a crack house. Really? The cops needed a warrant for this place? He noticed all of the activity next door and grinned.

He slowly drove by the address, going down the block, then taking a right and down two more blocks before he parked.

He checked his texts. There was an incoming from Lydia telling him to call. Dammit it all to hell, he wished he had comm equipment like a normal field op so he had Lydia in his ear.

"Yeah?" he asked Lydia when he called her.

"They're still waiting on a warrant, but let me tell you what I know about your address. The owner of this set of prints is Caleb Marks. He went up for stealing cars. He's been paroled for the last two years. This is the address he has on file, but when I did a little more digging, it's his brother's place. His brother is bad news. Gang affiliation."

"The parole officer didn't catch that?"

"Used to belong to their mother. She died last year," Lydia answered. "I don't think this is your guy. The gang is Aryan Nation, not likely to have ties with Mexico."

"They're not going to like seeing an Asian guy knocking on their door either."

Lydia chuckled. "You were planning on knocking?"

Raiden grimaced. "Probably not. Even though this doesn't look promising, it's one of the few leads we have, so I'm taking it."

"Understood. Your phone's on vibrate, right?"

"Yep."

"I'll call three times in a row if cops are coming your way, deal?"

"Yep."

"Okay, going to check in with Clint. Bye." The phone went dead.

Raiden got out of the rental car and popped the trunk. Before he'd left Lisa's house, he had finally ventured inside. He hadn't given a shit what it looked like, he'd been busy looking for her toolbox. Any woman who was a guide up in Alaska sure as hell had a toolbox, and he knew depending on what he was up against, he might be doing a little breaking and entering, so he'd need some tools. Raiden opened the box and grabbed a screwdriver, then he snagged a hooded sweatshirt and tugged it on. He also grabbed a pair of latex gloves he'd found at Lisa's and shoved them into the hoodie's pocket. The temp was in the mid-sixties, but in this neighborhood, most people didn't want to be seen so he wasn't going to stand out wearing a sweatshirt with a hood.

He wandered down the cracked sidewalk, going slow, taking in everything. It was an active Thursday night. A lot of trash cars, intermingled with cars that had tens of thousands of dollars' worth of after-market parts sunk into them. He recognized houses where the owners had been there forever and were doing their part to make a nice life for themselves despite the way the neighborhood had fallen to shit around them. Lots of bars on windows. It was a shame.

He was getting a lot of assessing looks as he walked by, but nobody was going to approach somebody his size. As he turned the corner to the Marks' house, he went on high alert. The first house he passed, which was next door to the Marks', was having a hell of a party, and Raiden couldn't be happier.

If Raiden had to guess, you just had to pay to get into the party. By the looks of it, anything went. He clocked the guy at the door who was looking at everybody passing in and out between the inside and the front yard, and Raiden would guess he was the one collecting money. He wondered just how many illegal drugs were being done inside, but at this point, he didn't much care.

The backyards were butted up against one another and Marks' house was dark. Raiden figured the easiest way to get into the Marks' house without getting noticed would be mingling with the neighbor's backyard party crowd and hopping the fence. He maneuvered through the teeming humanity leading up to the front door and tipped his chin to the guy covering the door.

"Fifty."

Raiden pulled out a hundred-dollar bill from his wallet. "Got change?"

"No," the guy said as he plucked the bill out of Raiden's hand. "Go on inside. Tell Chris that Bill says you don't owe for the first beer."

"Gee, thanks." Raiden angled his way into the house and

was almost knocked over with all the marijuana smoke. His eyes narrowed as he looked around and saw just how many people were crammed inside. How in the hell could they stand it?

"Hey! Who are you?" A blonde girl who looked like she was in high school asked as she plastered herself to his front.

"I'm old enough to be your father, is who I am," Raiden rumbled.

"I know, rad, right?" Her pretty blue eyes were dilated. He was so going to call the cops after he checked out the house next door.

He pulled her hands off his shoulders and set her away from him. "No, not rad. Go find someone your own age. Or better yet, go home to your parents."

"Okay Boomer!" she threw up her hand. "You're losing out."

Raiden ignored the girl and pushed his way to the back of the house. Goddammit, they were running out of time and he was more than likely on a wild goose chase. When he got to the backyard, it was worse than in the house.

There was no grass to be seen, just cement. He saw three kegs set up and a table in the back corner where people were snorting stuff off the top.

Lovely.

He looked to the right and just a waist-high chain-link fence separated the two backyards. Surprisingly the Marks' yard had grass and flowers. *Guess the mom had taken care of things before leaving it to the gangbanger.*

Raiden went to the side of the party house, ignored the couple who were actually fucking against the stucco, and slid over the fence. He took out his gloves and pulled them on.

He tried the sliding glass door, but it was locked. An easy fix because it was an outside-mounted slider. Raiden inserted the screwdriver six inches from the door frame and the door, diagonal from the latch, at the bottom, and pried upwards. He held on and then tilted the door a little bit until the latch lowered and he felt it release from the bracket.

He looked over his shoulder. Nothing had changed over on the other side of the fence except that young-love-on-stucco was over with, and the boy was passed out on the ground with the girl nowhere to be found.

Raiden let himself into the house.

It didn't take him long at all to go through the home and realize that no one was there. He did find three guns and a bunch of weed, but nothing that pointed towards Mexico or Lisa's kidnapping.

His pocket vibrated. Lydia. "Can this wait?" he answered.

"Clint has something, do you?"

"No. Give me three minutes and I can talk."

"Okay."

Raiden hung up and went out the back door, then jumped over the backyard fence. He saw two more bodies passed out in the backyard. Not good.

He made his way to the front door.

"Did you get your beer?" Bill asked.

"I got everything I needed to get," Raiden said as he left.

He was dialing nine-one-one as he walked around the corner. The cops needed to raid that damn place, like yesterday. He was done with his civic duty by the time he got back to his rental, so he started it up and called Lydia.

"What did Clint find?"

"I'm conferencing us," she said.

Raiden started the car and headed towards I-HOP.

"Raiden, so you got nothing?" Clint asked.

"Yep. Nothing. What did you get?"

"I made friends with a guy by the name of Rick Lopez. He's working for a guy out of Mexico. He's scared shitless of this guy. The guy is paying him big dollars—I mean *big*. But he also killed one of Rick's partners today."

"Does Rick know where Lisa is?"

"Not anymore."

"So he was part of her kidnapping," Raiden said as he passed by another car only to end up getting to a red light faster.

"Yeah, he was. He's now very sorry that he knocked Camilla to the ground."

"I don't give a shit about that," Raiden bit out. "Tell me what he knows."

"One of his buddies, the dead guy, was hired two weeks ago to kidnap Lisa. He tried breaking into her house but then ran scared. He ended up calling in Rick and one other small-time player. They got an idea, and the dead guy tapped a lawn care guy in Lisa's neighborhood to hook them up with times that lawn care is done so they could blend in. So they picked her up today, and their Mexican client said to sit on Lisa for the next two days, and he'd pay them the rest of the money when he picks her up."

"So where the fuck is she?" Raiden demanded to know.

"That's the problem, Rick doesn't know. They had her at a storage unit, but the lawn care guy said he and his old lady would watch her for two days."

Raiden shut his eyes for a moment, then opened them. The light was green so he started going fast toward the freeway.

"So we had four guys, plus the Mexican client. Then the client offs one guy. Now we're down to three. One of whom is Rick, who you have. Then we have the lawn care guy and his old lady who has Lisa, does that sum it up?" Raiden asked.

"No. The third guy, according to Rick, is named Sanchez. Sanchez is planning on cleaning up loose ends. That means he's heading toward Cami. I want to know where you are, so I can determine if you have Cami, or I do." Clint said.

"How in the name of all that's holy would he know where Cami is?" Raiden demanded to know.

"Rick told him to check the hospital because he saw she took quite the hit going down on the pavement."

"Shit. Okay. I'm almost on the freeway, about four exits from the hospital," Raiden answered.

"Then you have Cami. I'll go back to Lisa's place and see what I can do with Rick's information to identify the lawn care guy."

"Hold up," Raiden said. "Lydia, is Harry still there?"

"Yes."

"Put your phone on speaker."

"You're on speaker," Lydia said.

"Harry, are you up to speed on everything from Clint?" Raiden asked.

"Yep." The man answered.

"Call the cops and let them know the situation. Since I'm closest, I'm going to the hospital first, but get over here, will you?"

"Sure. You want me to relieve you?" Harry asked.

"Yeah. Shouldn't need us there with the cops involved. I'd just feel better if one of us was."

"I hear that," Harry agreed. "I'll meet you at the hospital."

15

RAIDEN WAS SLUGGING DOWN HIS THIRD CUP OF COFFEE AND the sun wasn't even up. He'd had a minimal amount of shut-eye. He was looking at Clint's laptop, trying to see if anything new had pinged on his search in the last five minutes. Lydia had told him what to look for when she and Clint had gone to bed in Lisa's master bedroom three hours ago. A.J. was asleep in the guest bedroom.

Raiden barely flinched when his phone vibrated on the kitchen table, but when he saw it was Kane McNamara, he pounced on it.

"What in the fuck has been going on?" Kane demanded to know. "How in the hell is my wife in Arizona?"

"She came with Carys. Hell, I don't have to tell you what your wife is like, do I?"

Kane sighed.

"So, what took you so long to call?" Raiden wanted to know.

"I've been busy looking over the shit that Clint and Lydia sent me. Didn't have time to hold your hand and sing Kumbaya." Kane's growl sounded refreshed.

"Don't bust my balls, and tell me what you've got."

"Talked to Captain Hale. Some of the Federales down in the Yucatan peninsula are in the pocket of the newest cartel down there. Maria Jimenez was busy sleeping with the guy who launched the kidnapping. You wanna know the name of the guy who runs the cartel?"

Raiden squeezed the bridge of his nose. "Something Jimenez?" Raiden guessed.

"Yep, Rolando Jimenez. Maria is his niece."

"Fuck."

"She takes after her uncle. She likes to slice and dice is the word on the street."

Raiden thought about the scar on Lisa's arm. "You know that we're on a time clock, right?" Raiden asked.

"Yep. I figure she's got to make her way over the border. She's going to want to get personal with Lisa."

"How good is Clint?" Raiden asked softly. He'd remembered hearing some rumors after they started working together and it had been weighing on him.

"You couldn't ask for better," Kane said.

"I heard that he was having some problems," Raiden said. "That head injury. I called him because his last name started with 'A' so he was the first name on my phone," Raiden admitted.

"I'm serious as a fucking heart attack," Kane said. "Clint beat that back. I don't know how the hell he did it, but he did. Probably with Lydia's help. I looked over everything he and Lydia have put together; it's spot on."

For the first time in hours, Raiden felt himself give a small sigh of relief.

"We're going to find the gardener," Raiden said. "We'll be knocking on doors here in the neighborhood this morning."

"Good call," Kane said. "Put A.J. on it. She can get anybody talking."

Raiden smiled. It was true, Kane's wife had a way about her.

"Clint has all of Rick's communication devices hacked, so if the gardener calls him, he'll be able to track him."

"What about the dead guy's phone?" Kane asked. "Wasn't that the guy who had the communication with the gardener?"

"Rick put him and his phone in a forty-gallon barrel of oil. It's gone. Lydia is going to tap into the cell phone records today."

"Good woman. Look, this will be the last time I can check in. Tonight we're going live."

God, he hated not being there with his team, but he needed to be here for Lisa.

"Raiden," Kane said sharply. "You're where you need to be."

"What, you can read minds now?" Raiden asked.

"Yes. Yes, I can."

Raiden chuckled. "Be safe."

"Always."

IT HAD BEEN JUST like the movies—the man had put some foul-smelling cloth over her nose and mouth and then she'd passed out. When she'd woken up, she'd had a pounding headache. Now here she was in somebody's trailer in the middle of nowhere, still with her hands and feet tied. At least the blindfold and gag were gone.

Lisa looked around, waiting for the panic to set in, the taste of fear to coat her tongue. She didn't feel it. Instead, she felt angry. Angry that for just maybe twenty-four hours, she had been eating and sleeping and beginning to feel like herself again. She had Camilla and Raiden with her, making her feel like she mattered, and she'd been seeing a light at the end of the tunnel, and now it was being ripped away.

She felt tears forming at the back of her eyes, but not sad tears, angry tears. Fierce tears. Goddammit, some gardener and his wife were going to hand her over to an evil bastard before she had a chance to get her life back on track? She bit her lip as she felt a snake of fear coil in the pit of her stomach, but she forced it down. She wasn't having it. No more fear, no more depression. That good and handsome Navy SEAL had stopped his life to come and help her. Her, Lisa Garcia. He said she was special. They'd discussed *Ender's Game*, and how the protagonist never let anything stop him. Even when the world was against him, he fought. She could fight, too.

No fear. Anger was okay. No fear.

She heard the door open and a woman stepped up into the trailer.

"Good, you're awake. I was worried my husband used too much chloroform," the woman said as she closed the door behind her. She had to be Nellie. She had smiled and spoken in English.

Lisa looked at Nellie. They were both Hispanic and about the same age, but that was where the similarities ended. She had to be about fifty pounds overweight, dyed her hair blonde, and was wearing a tube top that looked like it might fall off at any moment. However, this was the woman who had tried to convince Mel to call the cops, so she did have it a little bit together. Except for the part where she was in a relationship with Mel.

"I'm awake," Lisa confirmed in Spanish. "You might as

well speak in Spanish. I understood everything you and Mel said. I know that you're going to turn me over to that man pretty soon, and when you do, my life isn't worth anything."

Nellie's smile slid away, but she quickly rallied. "Then you also know I have to protect my kids."

"Once somebody like this guy has his claws into your man, he's all-in. He'll never let him go. You know that, right?"

Nellie swallowed. She knew Lisa was right, but she didn't want to believe her. She couldn't believe her, because then her world would be shit.

"You must be hungry," she said with a false smile. "Or maybe you need to use the bathroom. How about that?"

Lisa thought about it. If she was untied, she could easily overpower Nellie and get the hell out of here.

"I need to use the bathroom."

Nellie turned and opened the trailer door. "Mel, come in here. The woman needs to use the bathroom. I need you to guard her."

Lisa's shoulders slumped. Mel walked in. Nellie turned back to her. "Since you heard everything we said, you know we have to turn you over in good condition. We're not going to shoot you if you try to escape. But Mel here will definitely stop you, and he's big, my Mel. It'll hurt when he stops you. So don't get any funny ideas."

Lisa nodded.

Mel pulled a knife from his utility belt and cut the zip ties at Lisa's wrists and ankles.

"The bathroom is there," Nellie pointed down the short hall.

"I have to wait until the circulation comes back," Lisa said.

Nellie nodded.

"How much more time until you turn me over?"

"Tomorrow," Mel answered.

Raiden better hurry.

"ONLY TWO PEOPLE actually have contact information on their landscapers," A.J. said with disgust as she came back into the house. "The rest just wait for them to magically appear. One of them doesn't even know the guy's name. Said he doesn't speak English so how was he supposed to know."

"I don't really care about that right now, A.J.," Raiden said. "Just give me what you *did* find out."

"I've been talking to a landscaper who was actually working today. His name is Jorge Torres, and he's been working this patch for twelve years. He'd heard about the kidnapping, but he wasn't around to see it. I told him we're looking for someone who would know this area, probably worked it recently, and would have gotten involved with a bad crowd. Might have fallen off the grid recently."

Everyone around the kitchen table perked up at her information.

"I gave him my number. He thinks he can have intel for us within the hour. He told me that it was a tight-knit community."

Raiden pushed back his chair, knocking it over. He rounded the table and wrapped his arms around A.J.

She grinned. "Careful, big guy, I don't think you know your own strength."

"We should have Alberto's phone records in a couple of hours," Lydia said. "But your information might score before ours." She grinned at A.J.

"I don't care who scores when. I just want us to find Lisa and get her the hell home," Raiden said emphatically.

"How's Cami doing?" A.J. asked.

"She's fine," Raiden assured her. "Harry found an Airbnb that he was positive he could secure. He's got Carys and Cami there now. So they're safe, and Carys is watching over Cami, so she'll stay healthy."

A.J. nodded. Then she looked at Raiden and dropped her voice. "I know I shouldn't ask, but have you been in touch with Kane? I know sometimes you reach out to him in situations like this."

"Talked to him while you were asleep. Everything is fine."

She gave a short nod. "That's good. That's real good. I'll let you know when Jorge calls."

———

HE LOOKED DOWN at the book in his hand. He could hear the three people inside talking, but he couldn't hear what they were saying. It didn't matter—all he could think about was Lisa and that last real conversation they'd had.

He gently flipped the pages of the book, making a concerted effort not to do damage, even though he still hadn't released the rage he'd felt at her words from the other night.

Called me trash. Called me a slut. Said I was asking for it.

Those words had been circling through his mind like acid for hours. He'd tamped them down so he could focus on the mission. He'd needed to in order to ensure that he would get her back safe, and now they were so close. But in these holding pattern moments, he thought he would grind his teeth into dust.

Sixteen. She'd been sixteen when her grandmother had said those words to her. Had thrown her clothes out into the yard. That morning he'd looked at her bookcase, he'd seen some of the pictures—Lisa with some expedition up in Alaska. Her smile had been exuberant, like she'd just conquered a mountain, and for all he knew, she might very well have done it that day. That's who Lisa Garcia was. Kicked out of her house by some sour old bitch at age sixteen, after being molested or possibly raped, sent to foster care, and then she ended up climbing mountains.

He'd been so wrong that night when he'd talked to her. She wasn't fucking special, she was fucking magnificent. Why hadn't he told her that?

"Raiden! Come here!" Clint called out to him.

He shot into the house.

"Lydia got the phone records. Did a crossmatch with landscapers, and found a man by the name of Melchor Gomez. He's got a wife and three kids, lives in an apartment complex in Tempe."

"That's not where he'll have her stashed," Raiden said.

"Agreed. Lyd and I will start doing some searches of different properties, friends, relatives—"

"And I'll go pay a visit to the apartment," Raiden interrupted.

"What, and I'm just stuck going to I-HOP again?" A.J. bitched.

Everybody looked over at her. She held up her hands. "Kidding, I'm kidding. Tell me what I can do to help."

"We're going to have to hit the phones, as well as do computer searches," Lydia said. "That'll mean you."

A.J. nodded.

"Text me the address," Raiden said as he held up his cell phone and headed toward the door.

"You got it," Clint yelled.

Raiden was in his rental car in seconds. He had a good feeling about this. Not that she would be at the apartment, but that they were finally on the right trail.

16

I<small>T WAS A TOTALLY DIFFERENT NEIGHBORHOOD THAN LAST</small> night. There was a playground in front with kids playing there, and mothers watching them. Everything was well-maintained. It was just nice. Really nice. The Gomez apartment was on the first floor, facing the playground. Lydia had texted him that they had three kids, so he knew he had to go in soft and easy. Raiden put a smile on his face and knocked on the door.

A middle-aged Hispanic woman opened the door. She was holding a toddler on her hip.

"Hello?" she greeted.

"Hi, I'm here to see Mr. Gomez. I wanted to hire him."

She gave Raiden a wide smile. "My son isn't here right now. He's doing some repairs on my trailer. He's good like that. He's very responsible, my Mel. He's a hard worker."

As soon as the woman said trailer, Raiden was positive he knew where Lisa was. He felt it in his bones.

"That's what I've heard, Mrs. Gomez. That's why I want to hire him," Raiden smiled again. "This is a really big job, and it means starting tomorrow. Is there any way that I could talk to him this afternoon?"

The woman shifted the toddler on her hip and started to turn around. "Let me get you his phone number. What's your name?"

"Sato. Raiden Sato. And actually ma'am, I was hoping to talk to him in person. There's a lot to go over. I was hoping he could supervise this project," Raiden said.

Her eyes got wide. "Really?"

Raiden nodded.

"Then you should go out to my trailer. It's really out there. I own some land near Queen Creek, you can't find it on Google. Let me give you directions; why don't you come on in?"

He followed her into the tidy little apartment. Well, tidy except for the kids' toys strewn all over the living room. He saw two boys, maybe five and six, sitting on the couch playing video games. Mrs. Gomez put down the toddler who sat down on his diaper then crawled over to a plastic hammer and headed to his brothers.

Mrs. Gomez went to the kitchen bar and grabbed a notepad and pencil, then started writing down directions. When she was done, she ripped off the piece of paper and handed it to him.

"Thank you for this," Raiden smiled once again.

She smiled back.

"I'll give him a call that you're coming out there," she told Raiden.

Shit, I should have thought of that.

He looked down at his watch. "You know, I don't have time to go out there today. I'll give him a call tomorrow morning and set something up with him to come out to the jobsite. But that would be great if you could let him know that good news is headed his way."

Mrs. Gomez held out her hand and Raiden gave it a gentle squeeze. She was a nice woman, and the kids were cute. It was too bad her son, their father, was going to be going to prison.

He waited until he was in his car before he called Clint and let him know what was going on.

"Get to the house," Clint said. "Since I drove here from Coronado, I've got everything we need for an op. We can set up here."

"Get A.J. and Lydia to the Airbnb," Raiden said.

"We'll do it after we take off," Clint said.

"Do it now."

"Dude, I'm not sending Lydia away now. We're going to be figuring out our plan and she'll have input. She can leave when we leave."

Raiden gripped the steering wheel tighter. Every bone in his body said to protect women, but his teammates were pairing up with some of the most kick-ass women known to mankind and it seemed that Lydia Archer was in that same vein. What's more, he would bet anything that A.J. would have his balls in a vice if she'd heard what he'd had to say. Then he thought of Lisa climbing mountains. He bet when she got back into fighting shape, she would be the same way.

"Understood," he said to Clint. "I should be back in thirty minutes."

"All of us will be waiting."

IT WAS SWELTERING in the little trailer, and it was made worse by the fact that Nellie was cooking. She'd asked Lisa repeatedly what she'd wanted for dinner, and Lisa couldn't come up with an answer. Everything sounded awful, and she was sure she would just vomit it up. To make matters worse, her entire body hurt from when Mel had tackled her as she made a break for it and stumbled out the front door of the trailer, screaming. Then when she looked around and saw that she was surrounded by nothing but desert, she wondered why he had even bothered.

"You'll like Nellie's meatloaf," Mel said quietly.

"Kind of like my last meal, huh?" Lisa muttered.

Nellie and Mel looked at one another and didn't respond.

Lisa stayed curled up in the corner of the tiny couch, trying to think of a way out. Mel had a gun he kept it in the waistband of his pants. *If I could just get that.*

"Stop looking at my husband's gun," Nellie said as she laid out three plates. "You're not getting away. This isn't personal. We're trying to be nice here, you understand? I even made fresh peeled mashed potatoes to go with the meatloaf, not boxed flakes."

Lisa felt a red haze descend. "Are you fucking kidding me?" she burst out.

Nellie took a step back.

Lisa couldn't believe that came out of her mouth, but it had, and there was more where that came from.

She shot to her feet. "You're going to hand me over to the Mexican cartel, and you're talking about having peeled some goddamned potatoes? Woman, are you out of your goddamned mind?" She was vibrating with anger, sure that electricity would shoot out the ends of her fingers.

"Hey, that's not necessary, you—" Mel started to interrupt.

Lisa's hand shot up and she pointed at Mel. "And you, you pussy-whipped asshole. You need to shut your mouth. How dare you put your children in this kind of jeopardy? How *dare* you?"

Lisa took a step forward and stabbed her index finger into his chest. Once. Twice. And a third time.

"A man has babies, he protects them. That is his number one responsibility, then comes his woman. You are nothing. You are lower than nothing," she barked out the insults.

He grabbed her finger and bent it backward, his face a mask of rage. She felt her finger snap. Mel backhanded her and she flew against the wall.

"How's that for being a man, you bitch? You don't ever talk to me like that again! You got that?"

Lying on the floor, her hand curled up against her chest, Lisa shrieked when his boot kicked her ribs.

"Mel, stop!"

Lisa grunted when another kick landed, happy that she didn't shriek this time.

"You gotta stop. We're supposed to hand her over in good condition, remember?" Nellie was begging her husband to listen.

The next kick landed with much less force. Nellie's words must have gotten through to her pussy-whipped husband. Lisa coughed. She hurt. God, everything hurt, especially her finger. Then it really hurt when she grinned, remembering how she poked that asshole's chest.

"Here, let me help you up." Nellie touched her arm and pulled. Lisa flinched away.

"Just leave me here," Lisa said quietly.

"Can't do that. I need to get you cleaned up."

"Oh yeah, trying to make the merchandise look good," Lisa scoffed.

She heard Nellie's sharp intake of breath. Lisa felt another throwdown coming on. *Really?* The bitch was feeling bad about hearing the truth?

"Here's some ice," Mel said.

Nellie put an icepack on Lisa's face. *Guess I'm not getting any meatloaf.*

RAIDEN LOOKED across the moonlit desert. It was midnight and there was no light coming from the trailer. One white Ford truck registered to Melchor Gomez was parked out front. Lydia had provided the fact that Mr. Gomez had a thirty-eight Smith and Wesson registered to him. God knew how many unregistered guns he had.

"God, how old is that thing?" Clint asked, referring to the mobile home.

"I'm guessing it was built in the fifties or sixties," Raiden said. Even in the moonlight, it was clear enough to see it was pink. It was up on cement blocks and had more cement blocks for stairs. It was about forty feet long and there were two big windows at the front end and another two windows that could be seen from that side right next to the door. At the other end, just two small windows near the roof.

"Stupid not to be outside on lookout," Clint said.

"Maybe he's on the other side," Raiden pondered.

"Yeah, away from the road. That makes sense," Clint said sarcastically. He took in a deep breath. "But seriously, we're dealing with a total novice, with our hostage in a small closed-in area. All we need is one clear shot."

"I saw his kids today. His mother. I'd really like to avoid anyone dying tonight," Raiden said softly.

Clint nodded. "No kill-shots, got it."

They were ghosts as they made their way over to the trailer. Mrs. Gomez really needed to get herself a dog. Clint nodded to Raiden, and then Raiden carefully looked through the front window where there was a slit in the curtain. Lisa was curled up in a tight ball on a little pink couch that was built into the trailer. Her hands were tied in front of her, and her feet were tied. The bruising on her face was clear. Her eyes were wide open and she was staring down the hall toward the back of the trailer—that had to be where Melchor Gomez was. The door to that back bedroom was open, but Raiden couldn't see anything in there.

The side door to the trailer would press inwards and partially block the passage between Lisa and Gomez. Raiden crouched down to talk to Clint and explain what he saw.

"Go to the back of the trailer, pop the window to the back bedroom when I bust open the front door."

Clint nodded.

Raiden slid over to the front door. There wasn't even a storm door, and the door itself was a flimsy piece of shit. He counted to five in his mind, making sure he gave Clint enough time to get into place.

Bam.

His boot slammed open the door, and the whole trailer shook. He turned and crouched down, his gun pointed to the back of the trailer.

"Put your weapons down or I will kill you!" he roared.

He heard shots from a semi-automatic. Clint was firing.

"Gomez, put down your weapon," Clint yelled. "Don't make me kill you or your woman."

Woman?

Raiden looked over his shoulder at Lisa. She was looking at him, her eyes fierce.

"Raiden, get in here," Clint shouted. Raiden got to the small bedroom and saw the man and a woman standing by the bed, both naked. The thirty-eight revolver was lying on the bed. Clint was hanging mostly inside the trailer, through the small window.

"Oh for fuck's sake." He snatched up the gun. He wanted to get to Lisa but he couldn't leave them alone until Clint got in the trailer and watched them. "Clint, get your ass in here so I can get to Lisa. We need to take her to the hospital. Find something to secure them with so we can call the cops."

Clint was already out of the window and on his way to the door. When he arrived by Raiden's side, Raiden sped down the hall to Lisa and knelt beside her.

Lisa looked up at him, her eyes wide. "Why'd you say 'for fuck's sake?'" Lisa asked.

"Baby, look at you. Oh honey, what did they do to you? Tell me, what hurts the most?"

"Why'd you say 'for fuck's sake' in there?" Lisa asked again.

Raiden looked in her eyes and saw they weren't cloudy with pain or fear. There was actual curiosity.

"They were in there naked."

"Nellie and Mel? Both of them?" she asked.

"Man and woman," he confirmed, a little surprised that they were having this conversation.

"They're idiots," she said disgustedly.

Raiden pulled out his knife and took her wrists in his hands. That's when she hissed in pain. "I've got to cut the zip-ties, baby." He did it fast and then cradled her right hand. "He broke your finger?" he whispered the question.

"I made him mad," she whispered back.

He pushed back her dark hair from her face and saw the bruising there. "Is that why he hit you in the face—you made him mad?"

She nodded.

She didn't need his anger—it wasn't going to do a damn bit of good—so Raiden did everything in his power to dial it back. What Lisa needed was his help, his care.

"Where else are you hurting?" he asked as he cut the bindings around her ankles.

"Kicked me pretty good in the ribs. I think one might be broken."

He hissed in a breath. He was not going to be able to reign this shit in. "Fuck, baby."

"Found zip-ties. Going to tie their asses up for the cops." Clint called from somewhere behind him.

"He broke her finger and a rib. Tie him tight and make him bleed," Raiden yelled back to Clint over his shoulder, then he turned back to her. "Lisa, I've got to go get Clint's truck and bring it closer so we can get you inside and to the hospital, okay?" he said softly.

Her left hand flew out and gripped his wrist. "Don't leave me, Raiden."

Curiosity was gone, pain was there, and he saw her fighting back the fear in those beautiful brown eyes. She was magnificent. But if she needed him there to help fight back the fear, he wasn't leaving.

"Clint?" Raiden called out.

"Yeah."

"When you're done, go get the truck. I'm not leaving Lisa."

"Roger that."

Lisa and Raiden continued to stare at one another, even

after Clint left, not saying a word to one another, until finally, Raiden broke the silence.

"The other night I said you were special, do you remember?"

Lisa's eyes got wide. "I remember."

"Well, I was wrong. You're magnificent."

17

It had been a blur at the hospital. They kept her tucked in a corner behind some curtains before they'd sent her home. When she wasn't being examined, she was talking to the police. They kept at her for hours, until she saw Clint wrangling the detective's questions to a close. The cops were going to leave in ten, fifteen minutes tops with the way Clint was maneuvering them out of their chairs, but Raiden had had enough.

"Everybody out!" he roared. The two detectives' eyes shot to him.

"You've been asking the same damned questions eighty different ways for the last forty-five minutes. We're done here. Out!" Raiden pointed to the gap in the drapes.

"We're done when we say we're done," the younger male detective said.

Clint and the older female detective shook their heads, knowing that had been the wrong thing to say.

"Give me your badge number," Raiden demanded.

"Raiden, I have his card," Lisa interrupted. "His badge number is on it."

"Frank, we're going." The other detective said as she stood up. "Ms. Garcia, if you think of anything else, please call us."

Frank looked pissed but he followed his partner out.

Lisa watched as Raiden gave Clint a look, then he too turned and followed the detectives through the curtains. Raiden then sat down in the chair next to her bed. She watched him as he took in her finger that had been put in a splint and then his gaze trailed up to her face.

"How bad are you hurting?" he asked.

"The drugs are making me feel pretty good," she answered.

"You handled the cops really well." He kept staring at her face, but she couldn't get a read on what he was thinking.

"Thanks...I think."

"Lisa, this scared the hell out of me," he whispered.

That caught her off-guard. "You're a SEAL, this is what you do."

"No, I'm talking about this. *You*. You being taken. Not knowing where you were. It scared the hell out of me, Lisa." She reached over her body with her left hand and he took it in his.

He stared at her for a long time. "We're going to be talking about the next steps tomorrow."

It was like his brown eyes were magnets and she couldn't pull hers away from his. When she didn't respond, he gave her hand a little squeeze. "I'll take you home, people are waiting."

"Who besides Camilla?"

"There's Clint's wife Lydia and a couple of others."

Her grip tightened on his hand. "How many others?"

Raiden gave her a slow grin. "Are you the woman who

shoved her finger into the chest of her kidnapper and called him pussy-whipped?"

Heat suffused her cheeks. "Maybe."

"Then you'll be able to handle meeting a couple of new good people, I promise."

"Where will they be?" She just knew he was going to say her house, and it scared her to death.

"In your really clean house," he smiled bigger.

Her eyes closed and her hand began to hurt she was squeezing his fingers so tight.

"You can do this, honey. You can climb mountains. You're magnificent." His words flowed through her like warm syrup. "Open your eyes."

She shook her head.

"Lisa, look at me." She shook her head again, so he continued. "You yelled at those two fools. Got in their faces and yelled at them."

Lisa heard the laughter in Raiden's voice and she opened her eyes. "You're back, baby."

She took in a shallow breath—a scared shallow breath. "But I'm not really back. That was just the one time."

"Okay, you're on the path then. But Lisa, you have to know, you're going to be fine now."

God, I hope so.

"But people in my house?" Just the thought of it scared the hell out of her.

"As soon as the doctor gives the okay, I'm taking you there. We'll call in a to-go order at the Italian place, and eat. It'll all be good." Then he looked down at where she was gripping his hand. He tugged her hand up and brought it to his face. He made sure she was looking at him, then he brought her knuckles to his face, and brushed them with his lips.

Heat exploded through her body, and she gasped. Raiden's eyes didn't miss any of her reactions and she watched as his eyes darkened.

"We're going to talk tomorrow after everyone goes home." His words were whispered against the skin of her knuckles.

She nodded.

———

RAIDEN CLOSED the door after the last person left. Lisa was barely keeping her eyes open at the kitchen table that was now cleared of food.

"I liked them," Lisa yawned.

Raiden bolted all of the doors, then went over to the carport door and made sure all of those locks were set as well. "There is a lot to like," he agreed.

When he looked back at her he saw her heading toward the kitchen.

"What are you doing?"

"I thought I would start a load of dishes."

"A.J. already loaded the dishwasher, didn't you hear her bitching?" Raiden asked as he coaxed her back into her seat.

Lisa gave a tired smile. "I really liked her. She's totally funny."

Raiden nodded as he sat in the seat right next to hers.

"We've got to get you to bed. Did you hear Lydia tell you she changed the sheets?"

Lisa gave her a perplexed look.

"Clint and Lydia slept in your bed last night," he reminded her.

"Oh yeah."

Raiden relaxed. He couldn't believe this was the same

woman he'd been talking through windows to six days ago. But just because she had made such remarkable strides didn't mean she was well. Nor did it mean she was safe; Maria was still out there. Yep, they had a lot to talk about in the morning.

"So are you going to sleep in the guest room tonight, not out on the patio?" she asked.

"Are you comfortable with that?" he asked.

Her eyes didn't meet his, but she nodded. Not the resounding 'yes' he'd been hoping for, but he'd take it.

"Then yes, I'm sleeping in the guest bedroom." He smiled. "But I think you need to hit the sack right now. You look done in."

He stood up and went to the kitchen counter where there was a little white sack containing her prescriptions. He took out her pain meds and read the bottle. He poured out the correct dosage and dispensed a glass of water from the fridge.

"Here," he said as he handed the pills and water to her.

"You're pretty pushy," she said as she took the glass and pills from him.

"Yep. Now drink up."

She stared up at him. She didn't look mad, just contemplative. This was a good sign; hopefully, she'd still have that attitude tomorrow when he laid out his plan.

"Raiden," she said quietly after she swallowed the pills.

"Yeah?"

"Thank you for saving me." Her lip trembled.

He crouched down in front of her and cautiously brushed back a strand of her hair behind her ear. "Nothing and nobody was going to stop me," he whispered.

She leaned into his hand and he cupped her face. She

sighed—it sounded like a sigh of pleasure. "It seems like you've been saving me forever."

"Lisa, haven't you noticed? You're working on saving yourself."

Her eyes caught his. "You think? You think I have it in me?"

"I know you do," he whispered back.

"But you don't know everything. There's a lot about my life, and the things that I haven't done—too scared to do— that you don't know about me. I really am nothing more than a terrified child."

"The woman I know isn't that. She's kick-ass."

"I've lived my life with my head in the sand, too afraid to live." Again, her eyes were searching, trying to tell him something. All Raiden knew was that she needed his reassurance, and he would always give her that. Always.

"Lisa, you've lived a great life. The life you've lead has made you into the woman you are today. You're amazing. If you think you need to make some changes, then do it." His voice lowered. "What's more, I would be honored if I could be beside you when you make those changes."

"Okay, the drugs must be making me wonky, because this conversation is all kinds of too deep for me." Even though she said that she still kept her head resting in his palm.

"Then let's get you into bed. Everything will be better tomorrow." He smiled.

She nodded and he helped her out of her chair and walked to her to the door of the master bedroom.

"Are you good from here?" he asked.

She nodded.

"I need words, honey."

"I'm good. Good night, Raiden."

"Good night, Lisa."

Her golden-brown eyes stayed on his until the door closed between them. As soon as she was behind her door, he went into the living room and pulled out his phone. He texted his mom. They were going to need to talk first thing in the morning, well before the time that Lisa woke up.

18

SHE SMELLED COFFEE AS SOON AS SHE OPENED HER EYES, THEN she rolled over and winced. Lisa stretched her right arm over her head and looked at her finger in the splint and grinned. It might be broken, but it sure as hell had felt good jabbing it at Mel. Pushing back the covers she headed toward her bathroom—her *clean* bathroom—then reached into her shower and turned on the water. She glanced over and smiled when she saw only pear body wash in the rack.

Lisa stripped down fast, unwrapping the bindings around her ribs, and then looked at herself in the mirror.

I look like shit.

She leaned in over the sink and probed at her black eye. When she stepped back she could totally see the outline of Mel's boot in the side of her chest.

Fabulous.

Steam was coming out of her shower, so she stepped in and hissed. The water felt good and bad, but she was hoping if she stayed in long enough the good would outweigh the bad. She had to wash her hair one-handed, but it was worth the trouble. By the time she finally got out of the shower, she was ready to go out into the living room stark naked to get her pain meds. She wrapped her ribs as quick as she could, left her hair in a towel, then put on jeans and a slouchy sweatshirt since she couldn't manage a bra.

"Do you need medicine?" Raiden asked before her foot was over the bedroom threshold.

"God yes."

By the time she hit the kitchen, he had a glass of water and tablets waiting for her on the kitchen counter. "You're going to need some food with that. Would you like pancakes, oatmeal, eggs and bacon, or a combination of all of the above?" he asked.

"Pancakes," she muttered as she sank down on one of the kitchen chairs.

"Milk or orange juice?" he asked.

"Milk," she mumbled into the tabletop.

A minute later a glass of milk landed in front of her. She thankfully grabbed it and downed half of it. She kept her head down and waited for the pills to work for the pain, and the milk to make sure she didn't end up with a nauseous stomach.

She heard the sizzle of batter hitting a pan, then a gentle touch on her back. "You doing okay, honey?"

She looked up at Raiden. "Getting there. Just physical crap this morning, not mental."

"Good to know."

He left her and then she heard him flip the pancake. She continued to sit there, wondering what they were going to be talking about today. Wondering what she was going to do now. It was going to take a while before she would be back to her fighting weight to go leading adventures up in Alaska; those were the toughest. Maybe taking on a second-in-command position on some tours in Wyoming or something; she should be able to pull that off.

That's pretty much all that was left open to her now that all of her hopes of finding family in Mexico had turned to ash. But even doing that kind of light work was still going to be a bit much. She would probably need at least six weeks to get her strength back up after letting herself fall to shit like she had after Mexico.

"That was a long-assed sigh," Raiden said as he slipped a plate of pancakes in front of her.

Lisa looked up at him but he was gone, then he came right back with butter and syrup.

"What about your food?" she asked.

"I ate earlier. You're the one who slept in."

Lisa nodded, then started buttering her pancakes.

"What was that sigh for?"

"Just trying to figure out my next steps. Need to call Paula and find out when I can get back to work. The pity party is at an end, but I'm going to need to get back into shape."

Raiden sat down next to her, his glass of orange juice hitting the table beside her glass of milk. "Lisa, don't you think you might be running just a little too fast?" Raiden asked conversationally.

She shook her head, avoiding his eyes as she took her first bite of pancake.

"You weren't doing so well when I got here six days ago," he said carefully.

"I was a damned mess," she said in between bites. "Isn't that what you mean?" Again she didn't look at him.

"Yes. That's what I mean. I don't want to negate the huge strides you've made. But fuck, woman, two of those six days you were kidnapped. I don't think you should be mapping out your next career move."

This time her eyes shot to his. He was not sounding happy. He didn't look happy either.

"Raiden, this is who I am. This is always who've I've been. I get knocked down and I get up again. That's life. You just keep on, keeping on."

"I don't care how many damn song lyrics you throw at me, Lisa, this is the real world. Just because you feel good for a couple of days, doesn't mean you're good. What's more, the reason you're feeling good is that you've had people like me and Cami here to support you."

Lisa set down her fork and picked up her milk. She needed its calming effects to coat the sour feelings in her gut that Raiden's words had conjured up. She looked down at her plate. "I'm going to be fine. I appreciate the help. I do. But I'm going to be fine. You can go home now."

Lisa watched as her plate of pancakes was pulled out from under her nose and Raiden put his fingers under her chin and tipped it up to him. "If you think I'm going home and leaving you here after what we've gone through the last six days, you haven't been paying attention."

Her stomach twisted. She needed more milk. Maybe some Pepto Bismol. Anything that would ratchet down the fluttery feeling flying through her insides.

"Raiden, just say whatever it is you have to say outright, because it's been a long six days, and even though you can read my mind, I can't read yours."

"Give me your hand." He held out his hand, palm up. It was big and strong and she wanted to hold it, but she was scared. "Honey, give me your hand," his voice was low and coaxing.

Lisa put her left hand, palm down, into his. He laced

their fingers together. "I told you that you're special to me, remember that? I said it right outside there, on the patio. Do you remember that conversation?"

She did remember. That conversation was burned into her soul. She nodded.

"Eventually my leave is going to be over, and I'm not going to let you live here in your house alone. I want you near me. Do you understand?"

She shook her head. She really didn't understand him.

"Lisa, I'm thirty-three years old. I've never been married. Never lived with a woman. Had one long-term relationship that lasted eighteen months, but I knew she wasn't the one. I always said that if I ever found 'the one', I was going to do my damndest to make her mine."

Lisa jerked at her hand, trying to rip it out of Raiden's hold, but he didn't let her. What would he think if she told him that she'd never had a single long-term relationship? That she'd never even made love to a man.

"Raiden, you don't know about me. Fine, you caught on that life wasn't roses and lollipops when I was sixteen. But you don't know how I closed off and became the neurotic woman I am today. I'm twenty-seven and a mess. Not just because of Mexico. I'm not normal. You don't want a piece of me."

Raiden's hold remained gentle. His thumb was caressing circles on the back of her hand. "Let's be straight out, okay? I think what you're telling me is that some shitheel named Damon hurt you when you were sixteen. Hurt you so bad that the police had to get involved. Am I right?"

How did he know Damon's name?

Lisa nodded, loving the feel of his touch.

"Did you ever get counseling for that?" Raiden asked softly.

"No," she answered, her voice a whisper. She wanted to tell him more, but she didn't know how. His eyes were so warm and kind, so compassionate, but still, how could she say the words?

"Honey, were you raped?" Raiden asked.

Lisa shivered. Her shoulders sagged and her eyes dropped away from his. "Yes," she answered. When she tried to pull her hand away from his, he covered it with his other hand, his hold warm and comforting.

"I'm so sorry that happened to you." She looked up at Raiden when she heard the deep rumble of his voice. He sounded in pain.

"I'm over it now," Lisa rushed to assure him.

"I so wish you were, honey. I wish that with everything in me. But that's not what you've said, is it?" She listened intently to his solemn voice. "You've told me that you've been living with your head in the sand for years, with nobody getting inside the walls you've built around you. Isn't that true?"

Did I really say that?

"Yeah. That's true," she agreed.

He took a deep breath, then expelled it. "Is that how you want your life to continue to be?"

His hands were so warm around hers. His eyes so kind. He felt so safe. "I went to Mexico to find my father's family. I wanted to take a chance to find my people, to open up," she admitted.

He nodded like he understood. "Lisa, I want time to get to know you, see if you'll lower your defenses a little bit, and let me in. I know that's going to take some time, so I want you to come to Virginia with me. Let me keep you somewhere close by to me, where I can keep an eye on you and make sure you're safe."

Her hand jerked in his, but then she relaxed. "You do?"

"I do."

Lisa pulled back her hand and Raiden released her this time. She fumbled out of her chair and stood over Raiden. "Maybe after a month. Six months. A year. Maybe then I'll have my shit together and I'll be good enough for something like that, but Raiden, I can't."

Raiden remained seated, he looked up at her.

"You can't stay here. Maria hasn't been caught, neither has that guy from the cartel, and he knows you're here. You've got to leave. Nobody would have the first earthly idea that you would be spending some time in Virginia. You have no ties there, they wouldn't ever look to find you there."

Lisa sucked in a deep, shuddering breath. Her eyes skittered across her room, landing on her picture of the Alaskan glacier. "Then I'll go to Alaska."

"Honey, they know what you used to do, they know that's where you used to work. They'll find you up there."

Lisa snorted. "On an Alaskan mountaintop? Give me a break."

She watched as Raiden continued to stay seated. He looked calm and relaxed. Caring, even. "Come to Virginia with me. Let me keep you safe. Let's give you the time you need to recover. Let's give *us* time."

Lisa took one step back, then another.

"I don't understand. Where would I go?"

"Wouldn't it be great if you had someone like Paula to live with? Someone warm, loving, caring, and crazy who would make you breakfast in the mornings and make sure you took care of yourself. Someone who would butt into every aspect of your life because she cared so much about you? Better yet, maybe even have a family all around you?"

"Raiden, you're not making any sense."

"I thought about it. I can't have you live with me; that's not going to give us the space we'll need to explore our relationship."

"We don't have a relationship," she burst out.

Raiden stayed seated, just continued to calmly look at her. "All right, let's use the word friendship. Coming to Virginia would give you a lot of time to spend with Cami. She's seeing a therapist out there who is doing her a world of good, maybe you can see them too."

Lisa thrust her hands on her hips. "This is crazy. I can't stay with Cami; she's just starting a new relationship with Nic."

"I'm not suggesting you stay with her and Nic, or with me. I think it's important for the next little while that you're surrounded by good, loving people. So I talked to my mom and dad this morning. Mom's probably already bought fresh flowers for the guest suite."

Lisa took a step backward and looked over her shoulder to see how far she'd have to run to make it to her bedroom. The man was crazy, with a capital 'C'.

"I'm not staying with your parents."

Raiden smiled. "You don't know them well enough to know how crazy the idea is, and how crazy they are, otherwise you *would* be scared. Cami has been to my parent's house twice. She really loves my mom, so when I mentioned my idea to her, she thought it was great. She's already volunteered to stay over at their house with you for the first couple of days after you get there to help you acclimate."

"Raiden, you're seriously out of your mind. And what's more, you'll be putting them in danger."

"Already told you. Nobody will know where you are."

"Maria and the Mexican drug cartel will find them!" she wailed.

He laughed. "Not going to happen. You pull up stakes, don't leave a forwarding address. Nobody will be the wiser. It'll take a couple of days to arrange. Cami will be back home and you can call her tonight to discuss it with her. In the meantime, we can go about getting your house shut down for the foreseeable future."

Lisa took one more step backward.

"I see you moving away from me, but it's not going to work. Why don't you go put on some TV, or read a book? We can come back to this after you talk to Cami, okay?"

"I am never going to see this as a good idea. Just know that."

"I hear you," Raiden said. His eyes were twinkling.

19

Lisa looked around Akari Sato's kitchen and for the umpteenth time couldn't believe she'd actually let Raiden talk her into moving in with his parents. Sure, she thought she might have to give in for a day or two just to give him his way a little bit, but six weeks?

Lisa let out a sigh and two male heads looked over at her.

"What's wrong?" Max Hogan asked immediately.

"Are you okay?" Raiden's voice was concerned.

"It's nothing, guys. Just trying to get the recipe right," she assured them.

Akari's kitchen was large, but with these two Navy SEALs in it, it was feeling pretty small and she was feeling a little hemmed in. She looked over her shoulder at Cami who was seated at the kitchen counter and mouthed the word 'help'. Cami just laughed.

Raiden's mom bustled into the kitchen. "Get away from the food!" she yelled at Raiden, hitting his hand with her wooden spoon as he crept in for a crab wonton.

"No fair, you've been letting Max be in your kitchen for

the last half-hour, and you haven't hit him once," Raiden complained.

"Go out into the garage with your father and Nic and leave me with Max and Lisa," his mother said with a shooing motion.

Max laughed. "Yeah, Raiden, leave me alone with Lisa."

It was total madness. This was the first time that the Satos would be having a big get-together since she'd come to visit.

"Cami, don't let Max try any funny stuff while I go out into the garage," Raiden warned with a wink.

Lisa looked over to where Max was diligently mashing the Adzuki beans into a paste for the red bean mochi ball dessert they would be serving tonight. The silly man had asked Akari for a recipe a few months ago, not knowing that was not how she rolled. She didn't write anything down—all recipes were in her head. Therefore he was in the kitchen getting a hands-on demonstration of how to make the treats. He was actually doing a damn good job of it.

"Lisa, what are you daydreaming about? Stir the dough," Akari said as she pointed her spoon at her. Lisa was in charge of making the mochi, which was the rice dough that would surround the red bean paste. She heard Cami giggling from behind her. Akari's attention lasered in on Cami.

"Cami, I need you to get some of the ice cream from the freezer in the garage, we need to start making the punch now," Akari instructed the school counselor.

"You got it, Mrs. Sato," Cami said as she slipped off the kitchen stool.

"I told you to call me Akari."

"On that, Mrs. Sato," Cami said as she walked away.

Lisa saw how Mrs. Sato's brown eyes, so like her son's,

followed Cami as she headed to the garage door. Lisa had come to realize just how alike she and Cami were. Neither of them really had a mother figure to write home about, so they soaked up all the mothering that Akari Sato was willing to hand them.

Six weeks ago, when Raiden had first proposed the idea, it hadn't taken a lot of arm twisting for Lisa to come out to Virginia Beach. She realized she was a target, so she needed to get out of Arizona and Virginia was as good a place as any. She figured when she got there, she'd grab a hotel and take the time to figure things out from there. She'd thought wrong.

Raiden hadn't been kidding about folding up her Arizona residence. He arranged for her truck to go into storage, her utilities to be turned off and he only allowed her two suitcases. Then Clint Archer had arranged for a private plane to fly them out of Phoenix into Virginia so that there wouldn't be a flight record of her travel. It was a little over the top as far as she was concerned, but Raiden had just given her the side-eye, so she rolled with it.

By that time, she'd been talking to Cami every single day, so she'd agreed to at least meet Raiden's parents when she arrived. The rest of the Night Storm team still wasn't back from their mission, so Cami had come to stay with Lisa over at the Satos' home for the first two nights after she arrived. Raiden would show up each morning after running a million miles, then they'd all eat a gargantuan breakfast. That had only lasted for three days, then Nic and the rest of the team had come back home, and Cami was back to Nic's apartment faster than the speed of light. Unfortunately, a week later, the entire team, including Raiden had to go wheels-up. This time they were gone for four weeks.

"You two are doing really well," Akari said. "Max, it's a

shame you were away this last month. My friend had a niece I wanted you to meet. She came over for dinner two weeks ago. Remember her, Lisa? Her name was Betsey."

Max turned Lisa's way and raised his eyebrows in question. Lisa fought back a laugh.

"I've got the ice cream, Mrs. Sato. Where do you need it?"

Akari rushed over to help Cami, and Max bent over to Lisa. "So, should I be thankful I was on a mission?" he whispered his question.

"Absolutely," Lisa answered. She didn't know Max well, or really, any of the Night Storm team members except for Raiden. But even if Max was a terrible human being, he really didn't deserve Betsey.

Max and Lisa turned to watch Cami help Akari wrestle a large punch bowl. "How are you really doing, Lisa?" Max asked.

Surprisingly, that question didn't really bother her anymore. Even though she didn't know Raiden's lieutenant, she realized he was one of the men who had rescued her and Cami, and that he was one of life's good guys. Not as good as Raiden was, but still a good guy.

"I'm doing well. I like staying here. Raiden's parents are fantastic. It was good when Raiden got back last week. His mother and father missed him."

"I'm hoping you might have missed my boy a little bit, too," Max said hopefully.

Lisa felt her cheeks heat. But before she said something she didn't mean, she figured she would suck it up. She looked Max straight in the eye. "I missed him a lot," she admitted.

Max gave a slow grin. Oh God, the man knew. He *knew*! How could he possibly know how often she had thought of

Raiden Sato when he had been gone? How she had fantasized about the man day after day, week after week.

Max's eyes twinkled. "I'll let him know that you missed him."

"You know, if you'd just let Akari set you up, Betsey could have been home waiting for you, too," she threatened him.

Max held up his sticky red bean paste-covered hands. "I give, I won't tell him anything."

"That would be wise."

"How are those red bean mochi balls coming?" Akari asked. "It seems like you're talking more than you're cooking."

Max threw his head back and laughed.

RAIDEN WALKED BACK INTO HIS PARENTS' home, watching his lieutenant laugh with his head bent near Lisa's. He took a sip of his beer and strolled over and dispensed the two others he was holding to Max and Lisa.

"Thanks," they both said.

"So what's so damn funny?" Raiden asked.

"I told him about Betsey." Lisa grinned up at him.

"Good God."

"Raiden, you have to keep me clear of this shit. I'm telling you, man, nothing but desk duty for you if I get caught up in your mother's matchmaking schemes." Raiden watched as Max deftly rolled some rice dough around red bean paste.

"You shouldn't have asked for a recipe. It keeps you in her sights."

"The shit's good. How was I supposed to know that

188 | CAITLYN O'LEARY

asking your mom for a recipe would mean she would try to marry me off?" Max complained.

Raiden reached over Max and Lisa's prepping area to the drying rack that had the crab wontons. Lisa smacked his hand.

"Ow."

"Those are for the guests," she reprimanded him.

"I'm a guest."

"Go ask your mother if she needs anything more from the freezer," she commanded him.

Raiden stopped for just an instant, blown away by the sparkle in Lisa's brown eyes.

"What? What are you looking at?"

He reached up with his thumb, and brushed an imaginary spot off her cheek, just because he needed to touch her.

"What was that?" Lisa asked.

"You had mochiko flour on your cheek."

"Oh," she said softly.

"Gotta go help Mom. Save me some mochi balls."

She nodded.

He bypassed his mother and Cami and walked out to the front of the house. Tonight he was going to talk Lisa into going out on a date with him. A real live date, not this meet-up-at-his-family's-house bullshit. A real live date. But even as important as that was, there was something that was even more important.

He pulled out his phone and accessed his e-mails. He'd received one from Lydia Archer this morning that he'd immediately forwarded to Kane McNamara. He wanted to see if he'd gotten a response yet.

Nothing.

He hit Kane's number.

"Raiden, I'm still looking into it," Kane said by way of answering the phone.

"Look harder. Look faster."

"Your woman is safe here in Virginia, be happy. We're going to track down the cartel connection, and with the new information that Lydia just provided we'll track it down faster."

"Kane, I've got a bad feeling about this," Raiden said as he turned down the house path and started walking down the sidewalk.

"There are no bills, no nothing, tagging her whereabouts to Virginia," Kane reassured Raiden.

"Man, they broke into the storage unit with her truck in it."

"Again, all of that paperwork just points right back to her house in Arizona. We're good."

"Like I don't fucking know that, Kane. But you and I both know, that means they are still anxious to find her. That means we have to put a stop to them. I don't think we should be focused on the cartel, we need to go at the source. Maria."

Kane didn't say anything.

"Kane, you there?"

"Yeah. I agree with you, man. Right now Maria's a fucking ghost."

"Clint left me a message today. Said he's going to have an old teammate of his give me a call. His name is Aiden O'Malley."

"Okay," Kane said slowly. "What will Aiden give us?"

"According to Clint, Aiden has some ties in Yucatan."

"Wait a minute, isn't Aiden second-in-command of Black Dawn?" Kane asked.

"Yep." Black Dawn was another SEAL team out of California.

"You're telling me that he has ties with Mexican cartels in the Yucatan?"

"Clint didn't go into a lot of detail, just that Aiden would be calling me. I'll plug you in when I get the call," Raiden told his teammate.

"You do that," Kane told him. Raiden's eyes narrowed as he saw his Uncle Hideto's Buick coming slowly down the street.

"Gotta go, man. Party's starting."

"Have fun."

Raiden watched as his uncle parked his car a good eighteen inches away from the curb. He was going to have to figure a way to get his keys away from him so he could come out and re-park the Buick a little later.

"Hey, Nephew," his uncle called out with a wave.

"Hello, Uncle." Raiden grinned as he went to open the passenger car door for his great-aunt. She handed him a casserole dish as she smiled up at him.

"Has everyone arrived?" she asked in Japanese.

"You know you're always the first to arrive," he teased her. "You like making sure that Mom has everything under control."

She reached up and patted his cheek. "You're a smart boy, Raiden. Have you straightened Leif out yet?" she asked as they started to walk toward the house.

"He's a work in progress."

"You'll fix him," Uncle Hideto said as he went to the other side of his wife. "I like your Lisa. She brought your Auntie flowers when she and your mother came to visit."

Raiden's eyes shot down to look at the petite woman who was walking slowly beside him. He hadn't realized that

Lisa and his mother had been to visit Auntie Yui. Mom was making all the rounds.

"She talks about you, Raiden," the older woman said quietly. "Not a lot. But when she does say your name, she says it with love."

Raiden was so stunned, he almost tripped on the sidewalk. He waited for his aunt to say something more, but she didn't. He looked up to the front door of the house and thought hard. Yep, he really needed to arrange for some alone time with Lisa now that he was back in the States.

20

LISA CUT THE TAG OFF THE DRESS WITH FINGERS THAT SHOOK. She was going out on a date. A *real-live* date. She'd actually gone out dress shopping with a *real-live* girlfriend, so she could find the *right* dress for a *real-live* date. She looked at herself in the mirror hanging on the back of the bedroom door. She'd gained back the weight she'd lost, but she didn't look the same as how she normally did. She was normally a lot more active, so her muscles were more toned. Looking in the mirror now, she saw a softer, curvier body.

Cami had dragged her to the lingerie department, mostly so Lisa could give her courage to buy more sexy underwear for Nic. But in the end, they both gave one another courage, so that was how Lisa was wearing a new copper-colored bra and copper-colored panties, both with a lot of lace. She looked at the dress in her hands and sucked in a deep breath, closed her eyes, then pulled it over her head. She had to wiggle a little bit to get it past her breasts, and then get it to fall past her hips. She opened her right eye, then her left eye, then both eyes.

Lisa bit her lip and turned to the side. Was it too much?

She'd liked it at the department store—it didn't show any cleavage and it went almost to her knees. Yeah, it hugged her body, but it wasn't like her body was anything to write home about, so that was okay, right? Plus, it wasn't red or anything, it was the same copper color as her underwear, so it was understated. But still, it seemed like it might be over the top.

Lisa fingered the soft material of the dress. She was nervous. She wanted to look good for Raiden. She'd been imagining having a chance to be alone with him almost since the day they'd arrived in Virginia, but it had gotten steadily worse as she'd gained weight and talked to Cami's therapist. Her dreams had even changed. Twice now she'd had dreams of Raiden Sato, and in one of those dreams, he had kissed her. *Kissed her.*

She closed her eyes, thinking about that kiss, thinking about being in his arms. She shivered, thinking about how it had felt in her dream, wrapped in his strong arms. She hadn't even been scared; she'd felt safe, and shivery. Was shivery even a word? His hands had moved over her body, around her waist, up the sides of her ribs...

Lisa opened her eyes and willed away the picture in her head. She didn't have time for it. She had to make sure she looked nice for tonight. She gave her hair an anxious look. That was another new thing. Cami had talked her into not just getting a haircut, but a cut and style. Never in her entire life had she ever once considered paying as much as she did for this haircut. But looking at it, with the chunky layers and the new bangs, she had to admit the money was worth it. But would Raiden think so, or would he think that she was trying too hard?

She sucked in a deep breath.

"You *are* trying hard. That's the point of this, remember?" she hissed to her reflection.

Since coming to Virginia Beach she'd made a decision. She was going to start living life. All of life. She was going to suck the blood out of life's bones. Of course, as soon as she'd said that to Cami she'd scared herself to death and hadn't talked to her for three days. But after that, she'd talked to Cami's therapist, which didn't go all that great at first. But now Lisa was beginning to feel a difference. She was seeing life through a different lens.

Near the bed were some ankle boots with a one-inch heel. Hell, maybe one day she would even learn how to walk in shoes with a two-inch heel!

She glanced down at her cell phone on the bed. Raiden was supposed to be picking her up in ten minutes. There was no way she was going to sit down in the living room with Akari and William, waiting for their son to arrive, she'd feel too weird. So she'd just put on her ankle boots, sit on her bed and wait.

Her phone pinged.

It was a text from Cami:

TAKE A SELFIE

SHE CALLED CAMI.

"Why didn't you send me a picture?" Cami asked.

"I'm not going to send you a picture. That's too weird."

"I haven't seen the dress with the haircut. I need to see it all put together. You have to take a picture."

"Women don't actually do that kind of thing," Lisa protested.

Cami laughed. "You're wrong, women do it all the damn time. Wait until you start going out with Eden, A.J., and Samantha, then you'll really be in trouble."

Lisa didn't know if she was ready for that much comradery. She'd always kind of avoided it, sure that she wouldn't fit in.

"So are you going to send me a picture?"

Lisa heard the front door open. *Oh hell.* Her palms started to sweat.

"He's here, Cami." She hissed.

"Good. Call me tonight. Or tomorrow morning. Or whenever the date ends."

"Cami," Lisa wailed. She'd told Cami what was up with her.

Cami knew.

She knew all of her phobias. That she had never done anything like that. She knew that she wasn't going to go there.

"Lisa. Calm down, sweetie. Calm down. It's going to be okay. This is Raiden. Just let him take the lead and enjoy. Remember, he cares a whole hell of a lot about you, and he won't do anything to make you feel uncomfortable, okay?"

Lisa sucked in another deep breath.

"Yeah," she agreed.

"So enjoy yourself. You're beautiful. Have a good time. Call me tomorrow, yeah?"

"Yeah," Lisa smiled. "I will."

She disconnected the call and put her phone in the small purse she'd bought to go with the dress. She rubbed her hands together, then shook them out.

"I can do this." She smiled at herself in the mirror, then opened the bedroom door and went down the stairs to the living room.

RAIDEN TURNED around at the sound of Lisa's foot hitting the bottom step, and he stopped in his tracks. It wasn't until he felt the heavy thud of his heartbeat going into overdrive that he realized he was staring.

"Hi, Raiden."

He took the four steps necessary to be right in front of her. She smelled different. Not pear, she smelled like strawberries. Her eyelashes fluttered and he realized she was wearing mascara and even some lip gloss. She didn't need it. She never had needed anything—Lisa was a stone-cold beauty—but tonight she was a knock-out.

"You look gorgeous, Lisa. Absolutely gorgeous." His voice was a whisper.

She tried to look over his shoulder.

"They're not there. It's just you and I and we're leaving."

"We are?"

"Yep, we have reservations. I don't want to miss one single minute of time with you tonight, so let's get going, shall we?"

She licked her lips, and then he saw the worry in her eyes. Her hand reached up to touch her hair and he took hold of it, then stroked her palm with his thumb.

He felt her shiver.

Dammit. He'd forgotten. He was coming on too strong. He dropped her hand and stepped back, then he watched as she took a small step forward. His eyes narrowed as he reassessed. Maybe she hadn't shivered because his touch had upset her.

"You're going to need a coat tonight; we have dinner reservations on the water."

"Okay."

"Is it in the hall closet?" he asked as he stepped over to it and opened the door.

"It's the red one."

His brows lifted as he pulled it out. "Pretty."

"Cami talked me into it."

He set it over his arm and held out his hand. He watched as her eyes lit up and she took his hand. He laced their fingers together and tugged them toward the front door.

"It's an Italian restaurant," he said as they walked to the curb where his car was.

"It is?" she asked as he opened the passenger side door.

"I know you like Italian food."

She nodded as she got into the car. He draped the coat over her lap then closed the door and soon they were on their way.

"This is the first chance I've had to really talk to you, other than phone calls. How has it been with Mom and Dad?" he asked as he settled into the driver's seat.

"It's been great," she enthused.

He'd been keeping close tabs on her through Nic. Raiden had been pretty sure this was the right move, and according to Cami, Lisa was soaking in family life. Raiden couldn't think of anything better than to offer Lisa the love of his parents. After the life with her grandmother, he'd been sure this is what she needed, and he hadn't been wrong. Nic had also expressed his gratitude, saying that this had been a Godsend for Cami as well.

"Your mom is the bomb. I even got her on a couple of Skype calls with Paula. They hit it off like a house on fire."

Raiden thought about Paula with her crazy red hair and her trucker foul mouth and had a hard time picturing her getting along with his conservative Japanese mother. "Really?" he asked.

"Oh yeah. Paula had her granddaughter on her knee the entire time, and Akari fell in love. Paula was telling stories about some of the tours that we'd done over the years, your mother was fascinated."

Now *that*, Raiden could believe.

"Do you miss the outdoors, being a guide?" he asked as they sped along the freeway out to the water.

"I'm beginning to."

He slid her a sideways glance. "You never told me why you quit it all and became a tour guide down in Mexico. Seems like kind of a come-down."

She adjusted her position in her seat so she could look at him fully. "Let's save that conversation for dinner, okay?"

"Sure," he acquiesced easily.

She was silent for a bit.

"You can't talk about your missions, can you? That's what Cami told me, but I wanted to ask you."

"She's right, I can't."

"She also said that you leave at the drop of a hat. No warning. Sometimes in the middle of the night. Is that right?"

Again, Raiden's eyes cut over to her. "Yeah, that happens."

"Oh."

"Lisa, why are you asking?"

There was a long silence.

"Lisa?"

"It seems to me that Cami, A.J., and the others have to be pretty special women to be able to cope with that from their men," she whispered.

Raiden's entire body clenched and his fingers tightened on his steering wheel. He couldn't believe that Lisa had been thinking that deeply about his job. That was something he could have hoped to have talked to her months from now, but the fact that she was even giving it the slightest bit of thought now, amazed him.

"Yeah, honey. They're special," he said softly. "Remarkable, even."

He felt her body jerk. She got what he was saying.

Holy hell, he needed to kiss this woman. He saw the exit coming up and he took it. They were quiet all the rest of the way to the restaurant. As soon as he opened the passenger door, the breeze hit them.

"Let me help you into your coat," he murmured. She nodded her head. She wasn't looking up at him. Damn, they were back in the shy zone. He needed to get them back on track. He guided them into the restaurant and the hostess immediately seated them.

Lisa gripped the menu with both hands and he could see her knuckles had turned white. He reached across the table and tugged at the menu, pulling it down so he could see her face. "Are you okay?"

She looked up at him and gave him a scared look. "I said too much in the car, didn't I?"

He pulled the menu out of her hands and put it down on the table. "Lisa, I'm not sure where we're headed, but I laid my cards on the table back in Arizona, remember?"

She slowly nodded her head.

"I told you that you were one of life's special people, and I was bound and determined to be there for you. I told you that after only being with you for two and a half days. Does that sound familiar?" he asked fiercely.

Her eyes were wide and she nodded.

"Laid it out for you."

She nodded again.

"Just now in the car, you told me you were thinking about me. About us, right?"

She nodded again.

"So you laid it out for me, right?"

She nodded, and he smiled. "Lisa you can actually use words. As a matter of fact, it would make me feel really good if you did."

"Yes, Raiden, I laid it out for you."

He continued to smile. "I can't say where this will end up. But we've both laid it out. We know what we're thinking, what we're feeling. So, let's just sit back, you order some eggplant parmesan, and tell me why you took a shit job in Mexico, okay?"

She hissed out a deep breath and nodded.

"Words?"

"Yes, Raiden. That sounds like a plan."

He nodded.

21

LISA HADN'T HAD A DRINK IN FOREVER, AND INSTEAD OF having one, she'd had two glasses of Chianti. Raiden had stopped her when she'd requested a third.

"Are you watching how much I'm drinking?" she asked.

"Absolutely."

She had no follow-up question for that. Instead, she ordered dessert. Chocolate cake.

They'd laughed a lot during dinner. Turns out that Carys' husband was a nut.

"Are you telling me that he actually dressed up as a woman and sang karaoke? That did not really happen."

"It did. He'd lost a bet," Raiden confirmed. "He has really hairy legs; it was not a pretty sight."

"Was this before or after he married Carys?"

"Definitely before." Raiden's eyes were twinkling.

"Is that something you would do?" Lisa asked as she bit into her cake.

"What do you think?"

"Uhm, no."

"You think correctly."

"I'm having a hard time imagining Carys married to a nut," Lisa admitted. "She's a doctor and pretty serious."

"They're good together. They balance one another out. Plus, he's not a nut when it comes to her well-being."

Lisa frowned and thought back to something she'd heard in Arizona. "Somebody said something about him stopping her double shifts at the hospital."

"He makes sure nobody is taking advantage of her," Raiden said as he stole a bite of her cake. "He knows the difference between when she needs to be working and when they're using her, and a lot of times Carys can't see it. She's too giving. He doesn't put his foot down, he just helps her open her eyes."

The idea of somebody taking care of Carys like that made her heart melt. "So not a nut. He's smart."

Raiden nodded. "You're done with your cake."

She looked down and saw the empty plate and grinned up at him. "You're the one who ate it all," she accused.

"We'll order another slice to take home."

"We will not!"

Raiden called the waiter over for the check and put in an order for a slice of cake to go. She kicked him under the table and he laughed. Her cheeks heated. She couldn't believe she had just done that. It had to have been the wine.

He held her hand as they left the restaurant and kept ahold of it during the long drive back.

"Wait a minute, this isn't the way to your parents'."

"Nope."

Her stomach fluttered. "Are you taking me to your place?"

"Yep. Just for an hour, then I'm taking you home. I want a kiss."

Her stomach flipped over. "An hour-long kiss?" her voice sounded breathy.

"Yep."

"I'm not sure I'm ready for that."

"It'll be a soft kiss. A gentle kiss. A kiss you'll like."

Lisa's breathing stopped. Then her thoughts went wild. It was everything she'd hoped for. Everything she'd been dreaming of.

"Wait a moment. Why are you telling me this now? Are you trying to ease me into it?"

They were stopped at a light and his head turned to look at her. "I absolutely am. Is it working?"

She started to breathe fast, almost pant. "I'm not feeling easy. I'm feeling kind of excited."

He smiled a slow, sexy smile. "Then it's working."

When they pulled up to a small house in a quiet neighborhood, Lisa had finally gotten her breathing under control. Raiden held her hand, their fingers laced, all the way up to the front porch. He disarmed the alarm and took her inside. It was nice. More than nice. It was warm and inviting.

"I like your home," she whispered.

"I'm glad." His fingers went to the tie at the front of her coat and undid the knot. Now her breathing started to hitch again.

"It's going to be all right, Lisa, we're taking this at your pace."

"I can't decide if I want this to go really fast, or if I want to jump into your arms," she admitted as she looked at the floor.

He chuckled as he pulled her coat off her shoulders. "Did I tell you how much I like your dress?"

She shook her head, still looking at the floor.

"I like your dress," he whispered. Lisa had no idea what happened to her coat, it just magically disappeared. Raiden tipped her chin up so that she was looking up at him, his eyes were warm and brown. "It's just a kiss," he reminded her.

"Yeah, just a kiss."

RAIDEN KNEW LISA WAS NERVOUS, but he would bet his classic mustang convertible that he was more nervous. He had a good idea that Lisa had not had many kisses in her life. In fact, she might not have had any, and the idea that he was the man who was going to give her one scared him down to his toes.

She was uneasy, he could see that, but he could see the want in her eyes too. This woman, who had been through hell, was standing in his house just inches away from him, looking at him with want in her eyes. How had he gotten so lucky?

He cupped her jaw. His thumb traced her bottom lip and her body trembled. He put his arm around her waist and pulled her close until her hands rested against his chest. She melted into him. He slanted his mouth over hers and she stiffened, which was just fine. They had all the time in the world.

He drew his fingers up the side of her cheek and gentled his lips, brushing them softly back and forth against the pillowy softness of hers. Back and forth, he took his time, until finally, she started to follow his lead, moving with him. She relaxed again into his hold and he licked his tongue across her bottom lip. She hitched in a breath and drew back, her eyes wide.

"Do you like that?"

"I'm not sure."

"Come back and we'll try again and then you can decide."

He bent down and she reached up, moving her face closer to his, her lips parted. Raiden traced her puffy bottom lip with the tip of his tongue and this time when she gasped, her mouth parted more and she pressed closer. He moved his hand, gliding it into the lush strands of her hair, tilting her head so that he could pull her even closer, his lips brushing, teasing, and gliding against hers. Raiden pressed the tip of his tongue into her mouth for just a taste, and Lisa's hands moved up his chest, past his shoulders, and around his neck.

God, kissing her was like a double shot of whiskey. It took everything he had not to clutch her close and plunge his tongue deep. He felt sweat beading his brow, but he kept control. Then her tongue tentatively touched his and fire raced to his cock and he thought his head was going to explode.

He softly sifted his fingers through the silk of her dark hair, then kneaded her scalp, his tongue sliding against hers. She moaned and her nails bit into his neck. Raiden was careful not to press his groin against her stomach, even as she pressed her breasts tight against him. She rested more of her weight against him and he felt her legs tremble. Her mouth opened wider.

Raiden pulled back and bent, then she gasped as he put his arm under her knees and carried her over to his couch.

"What are you doing?"

"An hour-long kiss means we need to be sitting," he explained as he sat her beside him. God, he wanted her in his lap, but he didn't think she was ready for that. Then she surprised the ever-loving hell out of him and cuddled up on top of him.

"Lisa?"

"I want to be closer for our hour-long kiss," she whispered.

Raiden had been afraid his erection would scare her. Thank fuck, he was wrong.

She nestled onto his lap and wrapped her arms around his neck, her face warm with desire as she looked up at him. She opened her mouth to say something, but he placed a fingertip over her lips.

"I'm taking you home in forty-five minutes."

She shook her head so that she could speak. "You don't have to."

"Yeah I do, honey."

He'd never seen her smile brighter. *God, this woman.*

She pulled him down until his lips hovered over hers. "How much can you teach me about kissing in forty-five minutes?" she asked.

"A lot." He whispered. "A whole hell of a lot."

LISA'S BUZZING cell phone woke her. She rolled over in bed and looked at the time on her phone. It was just after six o'clock in the morning.

"What are you doing calling so early?" she mumbled.

"How was it?" Cami demanded to know.

"I need coffee," Lisa complained as she fell back against her pillows.

"To hell with coffee, tell me everything."

She really needed caffeine before she had this

conversation. Really, really, really needed caffeine. Lisa tried to get her head in gear. "Wait a minute, can Nic hear you?"

"I'm alone out on the balcony, freezing my booty off. Now tell me everything."

Lisa wiggled deep into the bed. No way was that going to happen.

"He took me to Santorini's. He bought me a piece of chocolate cake to take home."

"Oh for God's sake. That is not what I'm asking," Cami practically yelled. "I want details."

Lisa sunk even deeper into the bed and thought about Raiden's hands on her body. He had just touched her hair, her face, her back, and her waist. She'd wanted him to touch her other places, but he hadn't.

"What's second base?" Lisa asked.

"You're killing me," Cami wailed.

"That's not an answer."

"Your breasts, he has to touch your breasts."

"That's what I thought."

"Are you telling me you only got to second base?" Cami demanded.

"No, I'm telling you we *didn't* get to second base."

"Holy mother of God. Where were you, in his parents' living room?"

"No, he took me to his house. He told me he was going to give me an hour-long kiss."

Lisa heard Cami suck in her breath. "He did?"

"Yeah."

"*Oh. My. God.*"

"Yeah."

"And he didn't even touch your boobies?"

"Cami!"

"Just saying. So he kissed you for over an hour, and he didn't get to second base?" she whispered.

"No, he didn't kiss me for over an hour. He kissed me for exactly *one* hour. Then he took me back to his parents' house."

"This is unbelievable. Wait until I tell Nic."

"You can't tell Nic!"

"I've got to tell Nic. This is like the most romantic thing ever!"

Lisa sat up in bed, her eyes wide. "That's what *I* thought. So I'm not wrong—it is romantic, right?"

"Sweetie, it is *so* romantic. He's going slow with you. He understands you and he's going slow."

"Cami, I told him he didn't have to," Lisa whispered. "I told him I was ready."

Cami laughed. "That's even better."

"What do you mean? It's time—I'm twenty-seven, it's time to man-up. What's more, it wouldn't even be manning up. I really, really wanted to sleep with him."

"Lisa, this was so much better. I love that he didn't even touch your boobies."

"Would you quit saying boobies!"

Cami laughed. "When are you going out again?"

"Tomorrow night. He said he has to meet with his cousin Leif tonight."

"What are you going to wear?"

"I don't know, he didn't tell me where we're going to go."

"If it's casual, wear the red sweater and black skinny jeans. If it's dress-up, wear the green dress."

"I'm not thinking the clothes really matter."

"You're right. Let's talk about the underwear you're going to wear."

22

RAIDEN WAS MORE THAN A LITTLE ANNOYED TO FIND OUT THAT his cousin had tried once again to circumvent all of Kane's preventative measures. *What is with this kid?*

"I'm sure he'll be home soon," Aunt Kathleen said as she poured him a second cup of coffee.

"Thanks, Auntie."

"Are you going to straighten him out?" Tallie asked as she wandered into the kitchen.

Raiden looked over at his younger cousin. She had a lot of attitude and seemed to like to bust her brother's chops, but he could see that beneath it all she really cared.

"He's just rambunctious," Aunt Kathleen said.

"Ma, open your eyes. Leif is on a straight shot to juvie if he keeps this up," Tallie said as she moved deeper into the kitchen. "Everybody knows it but you and Dad."

Aunt Kathleen sucked in a deep breath then turned back to the stove. Tallie rolled her eyes and looked over at Raiden. "Do you need any help? Do you need me to toss his room?"

Raiden's lip twitched. "I've got this," he assured her.

"I'm willing to do my part. Seriously, I don't want some kind of ex-con for a brother, it'll ruin my rep."

"Tallie!" Aunt Kathleen whirled around from the stove. "You're out of line."

"No, Ma, I'm not. Leif is headed towards serious trouble and you should be damned happy that Raiden is willing to step up."

Aunt Kathleen looked over at Raiden. Her expression had changed; she now looked seriously worried. "Is this true?"

Raiden sighed. "Yes, Auntie. I was hoping after our last talk things would get better, but they haven't. I need to hurry things along."

His phone vibrated, he pulled it out of his back pocket and read the text, then frowned.

Shit.

He looked over at his distressed aunt and walked around the kitchen counter to kiss her cheek. "I've to go. You tell Leif I'm looking for him, and he better stop avoiding me."

She gripped his hand. "Will he be all right?"

"Yes. I promise." Even if he had to wipe up the floor with him, Raiden would make sure he got his shit together.

He swept past Tallie and gave her a wink, gratified when he saw her relax.

As soon as he hit his car, he put his phone on speaker and dialed.

"Is this Raiden?"

"Yeah, is this Aiden?"

"Yep. I've got some information for you out of the Yucatan."

"That was fast."

"Yeah well, it sounds like you didn't have time to fuck around, and I don't have good news."

Shit.

"What have you got?"

"Rolando Jiminez has connections here in the States."

Raiden thought about the guy who'd been coordinating the kidnapping of Lisa in Arizona. The one that nobody had been able to find.

"Yeah, we figured that."

"You know he has family here?" Aiden said. He sounded surprised.

"Who has family?" Raiden asked.

"Rolando," Aiden clarified.

Raiden stilled. "Nope, didn't know he had family."

"Well, he does. That's how he's distributing. He has a brother who leads a gang out of L.A., and that guy is wired in. Raiden, I had my uncle do a deep dive on this; he has cops on his payroll."

"Shit, Aiden, we had Arizona cops all involved in Lisa's kidnapping. They needed to keep in touch with all of us for the case."

"The dirty cops are in L.A.." Aiden pointed out.

"Doesn't matter, information spreads."

"You're right, it does." Aiden sighed. "My uncle is trying to get a bead on where that crazy bitch Maria Jiminez is. Raiden, even for the cartel, she's whacked."

Raiden started his car and backed out of his aunt and uncle's driveway.

"Aiden, I don't know you, but I owe you."

"I drink single malt."

"You got it."

"I'll keep you informed of what I find out."

"Thanks."

As soon as Aiden disconnected, Raiden called Max, who thankfully answered on the first ring.

"Please don't tell me your mother has fixed me up with somebody," Max laughed.

"This is serious."

Max's voice immediately turned sober. "Give it to me."

"Just talked to a guy from Black Dawn. He has connections down in the Yucatan and knows that Maria's uncle can get info from dirty cops in L.A."

"Fuck. That means he can get info from the cops in Arizona."

"You got it in one. Aiden, the Black Dawn guy, is checking his sources to see if Maria has made it to the States. In the meantime, I need to put Lisa on lockdown, plus I need to get my parents the fuck out of town."

"Absolutely. Ideas?"

"I'll have it figured by the time I get to their house."

"How far away are you?" Max asked.

"Fifteen minutes."

"I'll meet you there. I'll think of options, too."

"Appreciate it."

When Max hung up, Raiden dialed Kane but got his voice mail. "Call me. Lisa's location has probably been breached. Need some options on where to store her."

RAIDEN WAS FREAKING HER OUT. Lisa couldn't understand how his parents could be so calm. She watched as Akari was folding William's clothes and putting them into a suitcase.

"I'm calm because Raiden said he has this under control," Akari explained. Lisa looked closely at the undershirt that Akari was folding and realized it had actually been ironed. She was the bomb. "And anyway, we were planning on vacationing in Hawaii next year anyway, this just moves up our plans."

She folded another ironed undershirt, then started folding William's boxers. Yep, even those had been ironed. "We have family there."

Lisa looked up from the packing process to look at Akari's face. "You do?"

"Yes. Most of my family is here in Virginia, but a lot of William's is in Hawaii. We travel there every other year. My boy loves to surf, did he tell you that?"

Lisa shook her head.

"He'll teach you. You'll love it."

"I'm not sure about that."

"Nonsense. Maybe you'll go on your honeymoon to Hawaii."

Lisa's jaw dropped. "Did you just say that?"

Akari walked around the bed and sat down next to Lisa. "My son is in love with you, you know that don't you?"

Holy hell.

"Uhm, no."

Akari's gaze searched her face. "You will." Then she got back up off the bed and continued to pack her suitcase.

Okay, now Raiden *and* Akari were freaking her out. She had to get out of the bedroom and see what was going on downstairs. As soon as she hit the bottom step, she was blown back by a wave of testosterone. William, Nic, Max, Raiden, and A.J.'s husband were standing around the dining room table, and they all looked grim. As a single unit, they looked up at her and tilted their chins. William spoke first.

"Is my wife done packing?"

"Almost."

"Good, we have to leave for the airport in a half hour. I'm going to go check on her." He headed up the stairs.

Raiden broke away and came over to her. "Are you doing okay?" he asked.

"Not really," she answered honestly.

"It's going to be fine. We're going to get you somewhere safe, and then we're going to arrange for Maria to become a non-issue."

"What are you going to do?"

"We're going to let her come to us."

Lisa bit her lip. She didn't like the sound of that, but she peeked around Raiden at the three other men and then thought about Maria.

"She's not going to come alone," Lisa whispered.

His eyes looked hard and determined as he looked down at her. "We know that. Did you pack a bag?"

She nodded.

"I'll go get it."

RAIDEN HAD FELT one thousand times better when he left Lisa at the high-rise condo in downtown Virginia Beach the day before. It was on the twentieth floor and had top-notch security. And even better than that, it now had Ezio Stark inside. The men of Night Storm had arranged a schedule to guard Lisa until Maria was caught, and in the meantime, they had Raiden's parents' home set up so they could finally take down the bitch when she showed her face.

According to Aiden's sources, Maria had used one of her aliases to get into the country two days ago but then disappeared in Chicago. As soon as Kane got that information, he started working with Clint and Lydia to track her down. But it was Aiden who came through again. Apparently, Rolando's brother, who was *not* Maria's father, had caught a private flight to Washington D.C. He also had friends with him on the flight, which had been the same day that Maria had done her disappearing act in Chicago. That definitely escalated the timeline.

Raiden was currently across the street from his parents' home at the Beckers' house, watching every person and car that came by. He was in his old friend Chuck's childhood bedroom. It had been easy enough for Chuck to talk his parents into going to their lake house for a week when Raiden had explained things.

They didn't have any kind of ETA as to when Maria or any of her goons would arrive, so nobody else but Raiden was physically watching the house. Kane had pulled in some friends, so the electronic surveillance was topnotch. Still, Raiden just knew Maria was going to try something, so he had to personally keep watch.

As he monitored the street he contemplated his one and only date with Lisa. She'd been funny at the restaurant. He'd been seeing that more and more as he'd had breakfast with her with his folks, but it had come shining through that night. When she'd told him that she'd gone to Mexico to try to track down any relatives on her father's side of the family, he could hear the longing in her voice. It was clear that the idea of family was important to her. He hated the fact that she hadn't been successful.

Raiden's pulse started to beat faster as he thought about that kiss at his house. In his entire life, there had been nothing else like it. But that hadn't been what rocked his world. It had been that moment in his lap when she admitted that was the first time she'd been kissed since she was sixteen. He'd been pretty sure, but having that confirmed was like a punch in the gut.

Lisa had been knocking him on his ass since she'd

opened her eyes and looked up at him in that Mexican jungle. Moment after moment, he'd been sucked in deeper. He had no rational explanation for it, it just was. But when she confirmed that he'd given her her first kiss in eleven years, she blew his mind. Then there was the fact that she wasn't scared.

Tentative?

Sure.

Hesitant?

Yep.

All kinds of turned on?

Absolutely.

Raiden had been kissing for a hell of a lot of years. In his entire life, he'd never had a better kiss.

He looked back across the street at his parents' house. Goddammit, they needed to put a stop to this Maria bitch so he could get on down the road with Lisa. He had plans. One of those plans was convincing Lisa that he was the last man she would ever be kissing, in her life.

"WHAT CAN I get you from the coffee shop?" Cami asked.

Lisa turned to Ezio who was sitting on the couch, one foot propped up on the coffee table, his laptop resting on his knees. "Cami wants to know what you want from Starbucks."

"Coffee."

Lisa rolled her eyes. "What kind of coffee? Latte, cappuccino, espresso, mac—"

"Coffee," Ezio interrupted her. "Just black coffee."

"Coffee for Ezio, caramel macchiato for me."

"You got it. I should be there in ten minutes, depending on the line."

"Sounds good."

Lisa hung up and looked down at her own laptop. It was either that or pretend to read a book. Either way, she needed to do something to make herself look occupied in front of Raiden's friends instead of freaked out. Of course, if she looked freaked out, they would probably think it was just about the whole Maria business, not the Akari business.

Honeymoon.

The word whirled and twirled in her head until she was dizzy. How could Raiden's mom possibly be thinking something like that? She and Raiden had only gone out on one date. One! And they hadn't even made it to second base.

Lisa sighed. Akari must be desperate for grandchildren, that had to be it.

"You know, if you sigh like that again, I'm going to be forced to ask you what's wrong," Ezio said.

Lisa swiveled around on the kitchen counter stool and looked over the relaxed man on the couch who was watching her so intently.

"It's just the whole Maria thing," she lied.

"You're lying." Ezio set his laptop down on the coffee table and sat up straight on the couch. "What's really wrong?"

Lisa frowned. "Isn't that enough?"

"Normally yes, but that sigh was an I-have-man-troubles sigh."

"Excuse me?" She didn't know what else to say. Then Ezio smiled. Holy hell, he had a pretty amazing smile. Then there was that lock of hair that fell over his forehead. The man was hot.

"Did you know I have younger sisters and had to live with them all through their teenage years?"

"No," she said slowly.

"Yep. You have all the signs of man trouble. So that'd be Raiden, right?"

"Actually, it's his mom, she freaked me out."

Ezio's eyebrows shot up. "Mrs. Sato? She's so cool, how is that even possible?"

"She said Raiden is in love with me."

Ezio barked out a laugh.

"That's not funny."

"The man gave me a whole lot of shit about Samantha, so it's really pretty funny from where I'm sitting."

"Well, it's not." Lisa couldn't believe she was having this conversation. She never had personal conversations. Never, ever. But since Raiden came into her life, with all of his friends and family, she was having loads and loads of personal conversations. How was that even possible?

The buzzer on the alarm system rang. Ezio stood up grinning. "Hold that thought, let me buzz Cami up."

He went over to the panel near the door and depressed a button. "Cami?"

"Yep. I have your boring coffee."

"Great, come on up." Ezio pressed a button, then turned back to look at Lisa. "Lisa, everything is going to be all right. Have you and Raiden talked, or is this just what his mother is thinking?"

"Ezio, we've only been out on one date."

Ezio barked out another laugh. "Woman, he sat outside your house in Arizona for days. He moved you to Virginia Beach to live with his parents. Don't make this out to be that you're not in a relationship with him."

When the condominium doorbell rang, Lisa almost sagged with relief. "You need to get the door," she told Ezio.

He was still shaking his head in disbelief as he checked the peephole. He started to open the door when it slammed open. Cami was shoved into Ezio's arms as hot coffee flew everywhere. A huge man stabbed a gun into the top of Cami's head as Ezio's gun came upwards.

"Put the gun down, or I put a bullet in her brain," the behemoth hissed.

Two more men pushed into the condo, then they shut the door. Cami was whimpering and Ezio looked calm. Lisa had seen that look before on Raiden's face; Ezio was trying to figure out a way to get them out of this situation alive.

The man who shut the door stalked across the room toward Lisa, the other one went toward Ezio.

"Remember, no noise," one of them said.

Lisa opened her mouth to scream.

"You scream, bitch, and I'll blow her brains out," the huge man said. Lisa looked at Cami and she started trembling with terror. Then she heard a mushy thud and she whipped her head around in time to see Ezio falling to the ground. The man who'd been behind him was wiping the blood off the butt of his gun with his sleeve.

The man next to Lisa looked her up and down. He pulled out his phone and took a picture of her, then it looked like he was sending a text. The room was silent. Lisa jumped when his phone beeped. He looked at Lisa and handed her his phone.

Lisa put the phone up to her ear, knowing who would be on the line.

"You killed Leon," Maria said.

Lisa's eyes glittered with rage as she looked at Cami,

then remembered that horrifying night in the church in Mexico. "Yes, I did. I killed that monster."

"You're going to pay."

The phone went dead in her hands. She didn't know what to do next. She saw blood pooling around Ezio's head. She needed to do something.

"What are you going to do?" Lisa asked the dead air as she turned slightly away from the man watching her. She pretended to listen as she dialed 9-1-1.

"Raiden will stop you," Lisa said as she turned a little more.

"What is the nature of your emergency?"

"I'm being held at gunpoint—"

Then her world went black.

23

"Max, I can't get ahold of Ezio, Lisa, or Cami," Raiden yelled as he hit the freeway on the way to downtown Virginia Beach. "They've been watching Cami."

"Hold on, what are you talking about?"

"Back in Arizona, while Cami was in the hospital giving her statement, she gave her contact information to the cops. I've been concentrating so hard on the fact that Lisa gave her updated contact information to the cops for the investigation, I forgot they have Cami's address too."

"Fuck," Max whispered into the phone.

"Now I can't reach her or Lisa. Lisa said Cami was going to visit her today."

"Calm down, Raiden, the security at the condo is tight—"

"I can't get ahold of fucking Ezio, either," Raiden roared.

"Are you on your way there?" Max asked.

"Yes," Raiden bit out.

"We'll have your back," Max said. "I'll call you with details."

Raiden hung up and concentrated on driving. How

could he have been this fucking stupid? Something had been niggling in the back of his brain since they'd discussed the dirty cop angle, and he hadn't thought it through. He slammed his fist against his steering wheel, then passed a car on the shoulder.

Raiden's eyes narrowed as he concentrated on the snarl of traffic in front of him, trying to figure out ways to maneuver through the glut of cars so he could reach his destination.

His phone rang and he hit answer from his steering wheel. "Yeah."

"I'm in the lobby," Zed said. "I'm going with the security manager to look at hallway and elevator footage to see what we're up against. Cullen is two blocks away; he was at the hospital having lunch with Carys."

Shit, tomorrow was the day Kane's guy was supposed to have set up surveillance inside the condo. Why the fuck had they done his parents' house first?

"Okay, okay. I'll be there in twenty," Raiden told Zed.

"Keep it together, Raiden. Nic is on meltdown; we can't have two of you off the rails."

Raiden let out a long stream of air.

"I hear you."

Zed hung up and Raiden veered off into the shoulder again to pass a few more cars.

"That wasn't very smart," the behemoth said. Lisa looked up at him from the floor. Her face felt like it was on fire.

She turned to the guy holding her cell phone, the one who had knocked her out. "Maria isn't going to like that you hit me," Lisa taunted. "Knowing her, she wants to inflict all the pain herself."

She liked the fact that he looked worried. At least something in this damned mess made her happy. Lisa tried to sit up, but it made her dizzy and she fell back down onto her forearm. She turned to search for Cami and Ezio. She saw that Ezio was still lying in the same exact place on the floor while Cami was now on the couch, staring up at the third man with a look of terror on her face. He was yelling down at her.

"If you scream again, I will slit that man's throat, are you hearing me, bitch?" he snarled, spittle landing on her face.

Cami nodded.

"The cops are on their way," Lisa reminded the men in the room.

The man who had been yelling at Cami turned to her and laughed. "No, they aren't. Told them it was a mistaken call. They get them all the time. Too bad for you, no cops."

Lisa thought back to what she'd said to the 9-1-1 operator. There was no way they could have discounted what she'd said. They had to be sending help, right?

Behemoth jerked her up off the floor by one arm, nearly dislocating her shoulder, and threw her onto the couch next to Cami.

"Just sit here. Your hostess will be here shortly."

Cami reached out her hand and Lisa grabbed it. "Let Cami go," Lisa begged.

All three men turned to look at her. The one that hit her finally spoke. "No."

"Maria wants me, not Cami."

"Then she'll get a bonus."

Lisa's eyes darted over to Ezio. He needed to be in a hospital. Cami's hand squeezed hers tighter and she caught her eye. Cami glanced over to the door, then Lisa remembered. There was a panic button at the control panel near the front door. Somehow, one of them needed to get over to it.

Lisa jolted when the big man who'd had his gun shoved into Cami's head sat down right next to her and reached for the television remote. The TV blared to life and he started flipping through channels until he found a wrestling match.

"I have to go to the bathroom," Cami said. She pushed herself up from the couch.

"Sit down," the guy standing next to Lisa's laptop growled.

"I can't. I have to go," she insisted. He opened his mouth to say something more, then she leaned forward and let out a mini tantrum. "I have to pee. How am I possibly going to foil your plans if I go into the bathroom and pee?" She stepped around the sofa and walked wide around Ezio, then she lunged toward the front door.

The big man sitting next to Lisa had been watching Cami, and as soon as she made her move, he leaped over the sofa and tackled her Cami's head hit the marble floor with a sickening crack.

The doorbell rang.

"Ah, fuck," the man on top of Cami muttered.

The cell phone guy quickly walked past the sofa and looked down at the couple on the floor in disgust. He looked through the peephole, then opened the door.

Maria stepped into the condo. Her eyes took in everything and she turned to the man who had just opened the door.

"What the fuck is going on around here?" she demanded to know. Before he had a chance to answer, she bent down and shoved her face into the man who was just pushing himself off of Cami. "Get your ass up off the floor."

This was not the camo-wearing Maria from the jungle. This Maria was wearing a navy blue pinstriped business suit with a short skirt, four-inch high heels, and had a huge Gucci bag hanging from her arm. As soon as the giant man got up, Maria kicked at Lisa's friend with the tip of her red high-heeled shoe. "Did you kill her?"

He shook his head. "No, just tackled her."

Maria prodded at her again and Cami moaned, then Maria smiled. "Maybe I'll start with her." She walked farther into the room, rounding past the sofa, and plopped her handbag onto the coffee table.

"Somebody turn off that noise." She waved her hand toward the television.

The TV was turned off as Lisa watched Maria pull things out of the oversized leather bag. Maria pulled out a ball-gag first, then she casually threw a skein of nylon rope down onto the coffee table. Lisa pulled her feet up off the floor and curled them underneath herself on the couch.

"And I couldn't forget this, now could I?" Maria asked as she pulled out a long, sharp, curved knife. She ran her thumb against the edge and smiled. "Ah, Lisa, we're going to have so much fun today and tomorrow."

A loud hiss filled the air, then a deluge of water poured down from the ceiling. "Ow!" Maria yelled as she dropped the knife. Lisa hoped like hell she'd sliced herself. She heard a crash behind her—it sounded like the door was being broken open—but then Maria was pointing a gun at her. Lisa twisted her head around to try to see what was going on, but the water coming from the overhead sprinklers was making it impossible.

She heard gunshots, then felt the sofa cushion beside

her jump. She dived to the floor, damned if she would make it easy for Maria to kill her. Lisa screeched when somebody landed on top of her. "Stay down," a man yelled into her ear. It sounded like Ezio.

"How many?" she heard Raiden shout above all the noise.

"Three men and Maria," Ezio yelled back.

"We're clear," Raiden shouted. "Where's Lisa?"

"Cami? Jesus, God. Talk to me." Lisa heard Nic's voice drowning out all the other noises in the room, but she couldn't hear Cami responding.

"Get off of me," Lisa pushed at Ezio. "How's Cami?" she demanded to know.

One moment Ezio was on top of her, then he was ripped off and Raiden was standing over her, pulling her into his arms.

"Where's Cami?" She couldn't see Raiden's expression; water was streaming down his face. "Tell me where Cami is. He knocked her to the ground."

"Are you hurt?" Raiden's voice was hoarse. His hands were moving up and down her arms, then he palmed her jaw where she'd been hit. "Baby, how badly are you hurt?" He sounded agonized.

Lisa reached up and grabbed his face with both of her hands. "I'm fine. I promise you, I'm fine. How's Cami?"

Raiden pulled her into his arms and shoved her face into his neck. Lisa couldn't tell which one of them was trembling more.

"Cami's going to be fine," Ezio said behind her head.

Ezio!

Lisa tried to pull out of Raiden's arms, but he wouldn't let go. How could Ezio be up and moving when she thought he was going to bleed out and die on the floor?

"Let's move the women to the lobby and wait for the ambulances," Max shouted. "Zed and Asher, you stay up here with me to coordinate with the police."

"Raiden, let me go, I need to see if Cami is all right," she insisted.

"Goddammit, she's fine! You're the one that was kidnapped again by a psychotic bitch with a knife fetish." Lisa wouldn't have thought it was possible, but Raiden pulled her even closer.

"But—"

The sprinklers shut off and Raiden lifted her chin so he could look at her. "Lisa, you've got to give me this, I'm begging you. Please just let me hold you for one damned minute. I thought I might not get here in time. I thought I might never get to hold you again."

She looked into his agonized eyes and started to cry. Her arms twined around his neck. "I'm here, Raiden. I'm all right," she whispered.

"Thank God."

24

RAIDEN DIDN'T KNOW WHAT TO SAY. HE HADN'T KNOWN WHAT to say for the last forty-eight hours, ever since Lisa started talking about moving back to Arizona. He sat down in his parent's living room, looking at the suitcases that were next to the bottom of the stairs. How could this be happening?

"She's running scared," Cami had told him.

Scared of what? Maria was captured and now they could finally start living the life they were meant to live.

Raiden heard Lisa's footsteps on the stairs and looked up from his seated position on his parent's sofa.

"Hey," she said quietly. "I told you I didn't need a ride to the airport. I could Uber it."

He didn't stand up, he just looked at her. "I'm not here to drive you to the airport. Anyway, Kane canceled your tickets."

She stopped short at the bottom of the stairs. "What did you say?"

He got to his feet but he made no move toward her. "I said you're not going to the airport and your tickets to Arizona have been canceled."

He'd never seen her brown eyes so wide, or so pissed off, or so confused, but his Lisa pulled her shit together. "Would you care to explain yourself?"

"So *now* you're saying you'll listen to me? Finally?"

"I've been listening to you for a week, ever since that day in the condo. I've told you, you don't have to worry about me anymore, you're off the case. I'm no longer your damsel in distress."

He blew out a frustrated breath. "And there you go again, not listening. Instead, you're just spouting off stupid shit. I've told you and told you, I do not have a rescuer complex. This is not what I'm about. I want you, Lisa Garcia. You!"

She strode over to him, coming toe-to-toe, jutted out her chin, and glared up at him. "You don't even know me."

"First, that's not true. Second, if you feel that way, then fucking share yourself with me!"

"You didn't even want to get to second base with me. You think I'm some kind of wounded bird that you've got to take care of all the time. That's not me! Yeah, my life has sucked. Yeah, I've built walls. But I'm a lot stronger than you think I am."

Is she out of her fucking mind?

"Are you out of your fucking mind? You've survived three kidnappings since I've known you, killed one of the most notorious kidnappers in Mexico, called one of your kidnappers pussy-whipped while you were poking your finger into his chest, and you about beat the shit out of me when I didn't let you get to Cami the other day. You're Ender from *Ender's Game*, surviving anything that's thrown at you. If you were any stronger I'd have to call you Wonder Woman."

Lisa rocked back on her heels, then shook her head as if to clear it.

"You had to coax me out of my house when I was too scared to leave it," she whispered.

"So?"

"I was living in squalor," she breathed out.

"I'm aware."

"You were the first person I kissed in eleven whole years."

"I was the one doing the kissing, so I didn't miss that either." Raiden did his best to keep his patience, but it was a near thing. "Is there a point to this?"

"How can you think I'm Wonder Woman if I haven't been kissed and I've lived in squalor?" she squeaked out the question.

"Jesus, baby, are you kidding me? That elevates you to, I don't know, Cat Woman?" Raiden shook his head. "Super Girl?"

He slid his hands along her arms, then down so that he could lace their fingers together. "I look at you and absolutely see the strongest woman I have ever met, bar none."

She shook her head so hard, her hair went flying. He let go of one of her hands and smoothed her hair away from her face. "Lisa, I would love you, be in love with you, if you had the easiest life imaginable, great parents, and were queen of the prom. Swear to God. But I love you so much more, you being this woman who has gone through what you have and become this kind, caring, and formidable lady."

Tears welled up in her eyes. "You love me?"

"I've been saying it for weeks, haven't I?"

She shook her head. "Not the words."

He closed his eyes. She was right. Not the words. He was an idiot.

He opened his eyes and cupped her face, his thumb catching the tears as they slipped down her cheeks. "I love you, Lisa Garcia. Please don't leave me."

"You really don't want me to leave."

"Fuck no."

She stared up at him, searching. Then finally, as if she saw something that made sense to her, she spoke. "Okay, I won't leave," she whispered.

Raiden bent slowly, watching every expression that passed over her face. She pushed against his chest and he lifted up. "What?"

"I love you too, Raiden Sato. I love you so much," her chin trembled.

"That's a good thing," he smiled.

"I don't know. I want this so badly, I'm afraid it won't happen, that I'll mess it up."

"You're Wonder Woman, you're not going to mess this up."

"I—"

His lips covered hers, and she trembled as her lips parted to allow his tongue access. She melted against him and he rejoiced. Not giving her a second to start overthinking things, he swept her up into his arms and walked up the stairs to her room, not breaking the kiss. Even when he laid her down onto her perfectly made bed, his lips never left hers.

Her hands were in his hair, pulling, tugging. The little sounds she was making sent sparks shooting straight to his cock. He knew he had to slow things down, but fucking-A, he was *not* going to let her slip through his fingers.

LISA'S LEGS twisted against Raiden's, trying to get closer, also trying to alleviate an overwhelming ache. Raiden lifted his head and looked down at her, his eyelids lowered, his eyes glittering. She'd never felt so turned on in her life.

"Honey, we need to slow down," his voice was a low rumble.

"No," she didn't want anything to stop this feeling. Nothing.

He cupped her face. "Honey..." That's all he said, that one word.

Her tummy flipped and she bit her lip.

"Raiden, I'm feeling things I've never felt before, I want to go with it, I want to fly with you."

"And we will, but this is your first time, isn't it?"

She opened her mouth, saw his fierce gaze, then nodded.

"So we go slow. We make sure there are no ghosts, and if you have any problems, anything that pops up, you let me know, okay?"

A warm syrupy feeling filled her body. Not hot, warm, and oh so nice. Now she felt safe. *God, this man.* Then she peeked up at him under her bangs. "Now can we round all of the bases?"

She felt his body shake with laughter.

"I'm serious Raiden. You told me you love me. And you actually meant it, didn't you." It wasn't a question, it was a statement. He nodded his head.

She moved her hands, sliding them away from his neck, down his chest, wiggling further down until she started to pull up the sides of his t-shirt.

"Lisa—"

She bit his shoulder over his t-shirt and he groaned. She pressed her advantage and pulled his shirt up farther. When she had gotten it as high as his armpits, she started to stroke the warm silken flesh of his back.

"*Lisa—*"

She dug in her nails and scratched, and he groaned.

"Get with the program," she whispered fiercely.

He pushed up onto his forearms. "You have your bags packed downstairs, it's too soon."

"You carried me upstairs to the bed, it's the right time." She lifted up and licked his lower lip. This time he didn't groan, he plundered. Lisa's head fell back on the bed as heat overwhelmed her. Raiden's power was breathtaking, and she cherished it. She wiggled beneath him, moving her hands again to get to the button on her jeans.

"We have time," he smiled lazily.

"No, we don't. I'm burning up." She worked down her zipper. Raiden stilled her hands.

"You've got to let me take the lead on this."

"Is that some kind of guy thing?"

"No, this is a me-with-Lisa thing." Raiden bent down again. She opened her mouth for another kiss but he grazed her cheek, then kissed her behind her ear. His tongue swirled there and she gasped, her hips surging upwards. She clenched at his back. His tongue trailed down her jaw, then he placed soft kisses down her neck. Such soft kisses.

He lifted up again and looked into her eyes as he unbuttoned the top button of her blouse. She bit her lip as he stroked her breastbone, then he unbuttoned the next button, and the next until her smoke-gray bra was revealed.

"You're beautiful."

"You make me feel beautiful."

He pulled down the cup of her bra, then traced around

her nipple with his tongue. She started to pant. "Take off your shirt, Raiden. You're beautiful too. Please take off your shirt."

Raiden sucked the tip of her breast into his mouth and she started to shake. The sensations were earth-shattering.

"OhGodOhGodOhGod."

She felt movement on her other breast and it took her the longest time to realize that he was rolling her other nipple between his thumb and finger. She wrapped one of her legs around his waist, desperate to get closer.

Raiden finally lifted his head just a little and blew on the wet nub. She cried out at the powerful sensation heating her blood. Raiden knelt up and pulled off his shirt, then hauled her up, stripping off her blouse and bra.

"You with me?" he asked.

She looked up at him, dazed.

He smiled a slow sexy smile. "You're with me." He reached down and pushed off her ankle boots and socks. His right hand caressed the arch of her foot. She moaned and her hand went to his zipper this time.

"No baby, just lie back and enjoy."

"Gotta touch you," she said as her hands skimmed upwards and smoothed over his chest, pressing into his thick muscles. More heat pooled between her legs. Raiden pulled back again, but thank God, it was only to pull off her jeans.

"Panties too," she begged.

He gave her a considering look, then his fingers hooked into her gray-lace panties and slowly pulled them down her legs, one slow inch at a time, his tongue trailing along with them.

What was he doing? Did he want her to burst into flames?

Lisa was shuddering on the bed when she was naked, and he was kneeling in front of her with his jeans still on. She could care less about second or third or fourth base—a terrible, aching need was ripping through her body. Even though she was lying there nude, she didn't feel vulnerable, she felt powerful. Lisa had never felt so connected to anyone in her life.

"Lisa—"

"I want this."

Raiden's lips twitched. "Are you ever going to let me finish a sentence in bed?"

"Not when you're going to ask stupid questions," she sighed.

He trailed his knuckles along the inside of her right thigh and she cocked her knee. His brown eyes turned molten. He moved down to the end of the bed, pulling her with him, spreading her legs. Lisa gasped as she read the intent in his eyes.

Raiden leaned forward and licked softly through her wet folds. She held her breath, not sure what to think, what to feel. His fingers parted her lower lips and licked deeper and she heaved out a huge gasp of air.

Again and again, Raiden brushed his tongue through her sex. When she started to writhe out of control, gentle hands held her in place but he looked up at her.

"Are you okay with me holding you like this?" he asked.

Her eyes filled with tears.

Oh God, her man, so gentle and caring. "I will always feel safe and cared for with you."

He went back to touching, licking, and tasting, then his tongue lapped against her clit and she shrieked as she ground her pelvis against his mouth. She let out a louder shriek when he pressed a thick finger into her tight sheath.

"God, yes," she begged, her eyes shut tight as she spiraled upwards. His finger pushed deeper, then swirled, and her inner muscles clutched at him. Then she felt even more pressure as he added another finger. Her knees bent, her toes almost lifting off the bed as she tried to rise higher and closer to the sublime sensation.

"There's my girl," Raiden's hot breath whispered against her wet heat. Then he sucked her clit into his mouth, his tongue raking against it. Lisa screamed as her orgasm powered through her.

RAIDEN DIDN'T KNOW how he could feel so languid, so content, and so hungry at the same time. If he didn't fuck Lisa in the next ten seconds, he knew he would combust. He crawled up the bed and pulled her into his arms, stroking her hair and tracing lazy circles on her back. Her trust unmanned him.

He didn't know how many minutes or hours passed by, he only knew that he'd never felt better in his entire life. Lisa stirred against him, her hand moving, then her head moved and when she sucked his nipple into her mouth he arched into her kiss.

"Jesus."

She licked at his pebbled flesh, her eyes flashing up at him from under her bangs.

"What are you doing?"

"I want more," she whispered against his chest.

Raiden's eyes closed, then she moved to his other nipple as her hand went down to his jeans, unbuttoned them, then slipped under the waistband. He felt her hesitate before she touched the tip of his cock.

"We don't have to make love."

Her hand moved further, then she stroked her hand down his cock and he groaned. Her hand stroked up, then down, then he stopped her.

"Let's slow down."

"Let's not." He heard the need in her voice. It was real. His woman was with him.

Raiden got slowly off the bed and pushed down his jeans and briefs, watching Lisa for any sign of trepidation. All he saw was need. He pulled out his wallet and grabbed a condom and rolled it on.

She started to push up and he shook his head. "Stay there, honey."

She relaxed back on the bed. Her hands moved up to lie on either side of her head and she parted her legs.

God, she was killing him.

He laid down beside her and pulled her into his arms. "I need a kiss," he whispered against her lips. He took her mouth, deep, hard, and wet. She wrapped her arms around his neck. She made little sounds of need and soon had her breasts rubbing against his chest. Raiden groaned.

"Now, Raiden."

He trailed his fingers down her body to the heart of her. She spread her legs wider, her sex flowering open to his touch.

"*Now*, Raiden."

He watched her face as he slid his cock slowly inside the woman he loved. Gently, just a little, letting her get used to his presence. She tried to lift higher, but he held her still.

"My way," he commanded.

"Okay."

He pushed in a little further, continuing to watch the heat and passion wash over her expression. With each moan of pleasure, he pressed farther until he was fully seated inside her warm depths. Raiden had never imagined that something could feel so good.

Lisa moved her arms and then her nails bit into his ass. Her knees clutched his hips.

He glided out and she moaned again, then gripped him tighter, pulling him back. He watched as her eyes glazed over and her breath sawed in and out. He was so damned close. Her sex grasped his cock, making him crazy. He moved his hand from her hip and touched his thumb to her clit.

"Come for me, honey," he begged as he pressed down and swirled with his body and thumb.

She gasped. "So close," she whined.

He went faster, pressed harder. "Now, Lisa," he commanded.

"Yes!" She drew the word out loud and long as she reached her peak.

Raiden felt his spine tingle and his balls ache as he thrust one last time, arching into Lisa, and found a bliss that he had never thought he'd find.

EPILOGUE

RAIDEN LOOKED AT HIS COUSIN AND SHOOK HIS HEAD. HE'D only been suspended, not expelled. That was only because they couldn't find the evidence they'd been looking for—everything was hearsay.

"I fucked up," Leif said quietly.

Raiden didn't respond. They were sitting at Leif's parents' kitchen table. His aunt and uncle weren't home.

"Do you know how this started?" Leif asked.

Raiden shook his head, knowing it was best to let the kid talk.

"Mary. I wanted to help Mary with her grades," Leif whispered. "I liked her."

"What happened?"

"She didn't want any part of cheating."

"So you lost your chance with her."

Leif nodded.

"So why'd you continue?" Raiden asked.

"Why not? She wasn't interested anymore, and the money was good."

"She's really not going to be impressed with the suspension," Raiden said.

"It's too late, she's dating someone else."

"God, kid, you're smart, you've got parents who love you, and that's a big deal, trust me; I know people who've grown up without that. You've got a good life ahead of you. Don't blow it."

"My parents are really disappointed in me. Especially Ma."

"So do better."

"It's not that easy," Leif said as he ran his fingernail against the tablecloth.

"Yes, it is. You pull your head out of your ass and you do better."

"But—"

"Leif, I don't have time for this shit. Got things to do." Raiden stood up and leaned over, fists on the table. "Do. Better."

Raiden watched as Leif swallowed. He searched Raiden's eyes. "I will. I promise."

———

THE HOUSE WAS dark when Raiden pulled into the garage. He was not in the best of moods. He knew that Lisa was going to be taking a group on a tour in Wyoming next week then volunteering with the foster home in Arizona and he was already missing her, and now she wasn't even home.

He got out of his car and closed the garage door, trying to figure out where she might be. Hell, these days it was a crapshoot. In the last five months since moving here, she'd bonded with damn near all of the Night Storm women and Raiden couldn't be happier. This was exactly what had been missing in her life, and every day he thanked God that she'd been given these blessings.

He hit the light in the kitchen as he got in the door, then he noticed a dim glow coming from the dining room.

What the hell?

He prowled to the other room, and stopped, and took a long moment to soak in the scene. A long, long moment.

His dining room table had been transformed. It was covered with a white tablecloth, there were lit candles, gleaming glassware, silver and china that he was pretty sure was his mother's, a bunch of covered dishes.

And Lisa standing at the far end in a pink negligee, garters, stockings, and high heels—well, two-inch heels—but he'd take it.

"Aren't you going to say something?" she asked nervously.

"Don't think I can." He circled the table and stopped inches in front of her. "To what do I owe this honor?"

"I'm going away for ten days."

"I'm aware."

"I'm going miss you," she said as her arms reached up to circle his neck. He stepped back a step.

"Uh-uh. Let me soak this in, baby."

"There's another reason I did this," she whispered.

Raiden looked up from her legs and looked into her eyes.

"Yeah?"

"I thought I was whole before. I thought I had finally made it, but in these last few months with you, making friends, going back to work, making love with you every night, I'm the person I always should have been. I'm me."

Thank God.

"Are you going to say something?"

"Dinner's going to have to wait."

Lisa giggled.

"Kind of figured that. The covered dishes are for show; the food's in the fridge waiting to be heated up."

"Smart girl."

Raiden bent low and picked Lisa up. *Now*, he could start planning the honeymoon in Hawaii.

FOR LIEUTENANT MAX HOGAN'S story check out Her Righteous Protector (Book #8)

ABOUT THE AUTHOR

Caitlyn O'Leary is a USA Bestselling Author, #1 Amazon Bestselling Author and a Golden Quill Recipient from Book Viral in 2015. Hampered with a mild form of dyslexia she began memorizing books at an early age until her grandmother, the English teacher, took the time to teach her to read -- then she never stopped. She began re-writing alternate endings for her Trixie Belden books into happily-ever-afters with Trixie's platonic friend Jim. When she was home with pneumonia at twelve, she read the entire set of World Book Encyclopedias -- a little more challenging to end those happily.

Caitlyn loves writing about Alpha males with strong heroines who keep the men on their toes. There is plenty of action, suspense and humor in her books. She is never shy about tackling some of today's tough and relevant issues.

In addition to being an award-winning author of romantic suspense novels, she is a devoted aunt, an avid reader, a former corporate executive for a Fortune 100 company, and totally in love with her husband of soon-to-be twenty years.

She recently moved back home to the Pacific Northwest from Southern California. She is so happy to see the seasons again; rain, rain and more rain. She has a large fan group on Facebook and through her e-mail list. Caitlyn is known for telling her "Caitlyn Factors", where she relates her little and big life's screw-ups. The list is long. She loves hearing and connecting with her fans on a daily basis.

Keep up with Caitlyn O'Leary:

Website: www.caitlynoleary.com
FB Reader Group: http://bit.ly/2NUZVjF
Email: caitlyn@caitlynoleary.com
Newsletter: http://bit.ly/1WIhRup

facebook.com/Caitlyn-OLeary-Author-638771522866740

twitter.com/CaitlynOLearyNA

instagram.com/caitlynoleary_author

amazon.com/author/caitlynoleary

bookbub.com/authors/caitlyn-o-leary

goodreads.com/CaitlynOLeary

pinterest.com/caitlynoleary35

ALSO BY CAITLYN O'LEARY

Her Unbroken Seal (Book #11)

Made in the USA
Las Vegas, NV
19 August 2023

76319172R00144